A ROSE FOR THE SURGEON

When Anna went back to the Princess Beatrice Hospital, more than ghosts from the past awaited her. Rob Delaney, the man who had broken her heart, had returned to haunt her – but was he the man who had sent her red roses? And if he hadn't, who had?

A ROSE FOR THE SURGEON

BY

LISA COOPER

MILLS & BOON LIMITED
London · Sydney · Toronto

First published in Great Britain 1979
by Mills & Boon Limited, 17–19 Foley Street,
London W1A 1DR

ISBN 0 263 73207 X

Filmset in 11 on 12pt Baskerville

*Made and printed in Great Britain by
C. Nicholls & Company Ltd.,
The Philips Park Press, Manchester*

CHAPTER ONE

ANNA glanced back at the taxi and her uneasiness returned. The huge wrought-iron gates on the northern side of the hospital were wide open and the driveway deserted, and there was no reason why she should not pick up her holdall and walk calmly up to the lodge and ask the porter the way to Matron's office.

But there was every reason. As the taxi disappeared and the last link with her journey from Somerset broke, it was like an overwhelming shock of times remembered, half-forgotten incidents that crowded back into her mind; disturbing, unhappy memories that after two years should have been put aside in lavender or ruthlessly destroyed.

Slowly she passed between the tall gate-posts and trod the familiar path once more. The untidy bushes flanking the driveway were dripping with the last of the dawn rain and a smell that could only have come from this place made her nostrils twitch and a slight smile touch her set lips. If she had come with her eyes closed and breathed deeply, that smell would have told her that she was in the grounds of the Princess Beatrice Hospital in south-east London. The winter smell of decayed leaves and soot, and an unpleasant and lingering haze of smoke from the incinerator behind the utility block, where the hospital authorities imagined it was out of sight and therefore, out of mind . . . and scent, had such a characteristic pungency that surely it must be exclusive to Beattie's!

Anna tugged at one end of her long bright scarf and

shivered. She looked at her watch and braced her shoulders as her stride lengthened, the long, slim legs in the well-cut trousers taking her nearer and nearer to the small door. She paused a few yards away from the door to check her makeup, trying to gain confidence from the sight of her neat appearance. A bit pale round the edges, she thought, and sighed, wishing that she had never considered coming back to Beattie's.

"I know you." She looked up, startled. "Don't tell me . . . you were here under the old matron . . . let me see, she left last year. It must be longer than that but you look just the same. It's Nurse Boswell. Never forget the pretty ones!"

"Hello Claud. It's good to see you again."

"Well, cheer up, Nurse. Where's that nice smile? You coming back to work here?"

Anna smiled and relaxed. Dear old Claud; at least he was a welcome bit of the past. No one knew his real name, but everyone called him Claud. He would wink and say it was a legacy from a rich uncle from Peckham Rye and, even after completing her nursing training, Anna had not found out a thing about the porter except that he lived alone in a small flat not far from the hospital. She looked up at the pale stone of the new block. "You'll have to tell me where I'm to find Matron," she said. "Is she in the new part or do I go to the old office?"

"Same old place. The new block is surgical. New wards, new theatre, new staff." He looked disgusted. "Too much blooming new everything, if you ask me." He eyed her with keen speculation. "I doubt if you'll know many of them there, but it depends where you're working."

Anna smiled. Claud kept his affairs to himself, but he had been the fount of all gossip in the old days. She knew that five minutes after she left the lodge, he would be spreading the news that Nurse Boswell was back, where she was to work, and, if he could winkle it out of her, the reason for her return. He would add details of what she was wearing and what she had done with her life during the two years since Beattie's last saw her.

"I have to see the powers-that-be before I know where I shall work; that is, if they want me. The new matron might take an instant dislike to me. Who is she? Anyone I know?" The question was casual, but Anna waited with some anxiety for the reply. The old matron had been kind and very considerate when Anna had gone to her in tears, pleading to be allowed to leave without notice. The older woman had told her that it was impossible to go without giving a month's notice, even though she had finished her training and was booked to go to Edinburgh to do midwifery in two months; but half an hour after Anna had gone to her room to try to regain her composure, a message had come telling her to report to Sister Tutor in the preliminary training school in Dulwich. It was obviously Matron's way of bending the rules, and it had given Anna time to recover, to become thoroughly bored by helping Sister to get the school ready for the next batch of student nurses. But it had saved her self-respect and given her a much-needed breathing space.

Fleetingly, *his* face flashed before her mind, the lock of fair hair falling over his brow; the face she had loved, and the man she had believed loved her as deeply. Firmly, she fixed her attention on Claud. "I forget who

7

was next on the ladder for promotion, or did they bring in an outsider?"

"Thought you would have heard. They upgraded Miss Joyce from Admin." Anna grinned. "You may smile, Nurse, but she isn't half bad. Didn't I say that she would make a good matron?"

"No, you didn't. I seem to recall that you and she didn't see eye to eye." He looked uncomfortable. "Don't look so worried. I know you had some trouble once but that's all in the past. Miss Joyce must have forgotten it or you'd never have lasted here."

"I must have been mad, Nurse. The others took things, and I thought no one would miss a few tins of milk. Learned my lesson then, I can tell you."

"It was none of my business then and it's not now," Anna assured him.

"Ah, but you stood up for me. . . . I heard about it."

"Well, Claud, you were always ready to help us juniors out if we needed things fetched in a hurry." She smiled. "Usually when we'd forgotten to bring extra drums up to the wards."

"Cuts both ways, don't it? There's some I wouldn't lift a matchbox to help." He grinned. "No names, no pack-drill."

Anna smiled. "I must check who is left of the old crowd. Do you know if any of my year are still at Beattie's? It's amazing how we lost touch with some of them."

"Nurses or doctors?"

"I should think all the house surgeons have gone on to better things."

"Like Dr. Delaney? He went to Ireland and took a job there." He looked puzzled. "I thought you knew."

8

"I heard he left to get married," she said, her expression giving away nothing of the relief she felt to know that Rob Delaney was safely across the patch of rough water called the Irish Sea.

"Married?" said Claud as he watched her walk up the path and run lightly into the building. "You don't know the half of it, ducks," he said softly. "All I hope is that you never have to see Dr. blooming Delaney again." He lifted the telephone receiver and spoke to the secretary in Matron's office, and when Anna arrived, slightly breathless, the girl was waiting for her with a welcoming smile.

"Matron is ready for you," she said.

"Am I late?" gasped Anna.

"No, you're five minutes early, but one appointment was cancelled. I'll tell her you're here."

A minute later, Anna sat on the same worn wooden chair that the other Anna had used; but this time the girl sat erect, her piquant face smiling. The old ghosts slumbered, and the room had been re-decorated since her last visit. A bowl of early daffodils sat on the broad desk and pot-plants relieved the severity of the long window sills. It was a prettier room now, with an air of taste and comfort that had been lacking in the old days. Matron – no one, Anna noticed, called her the Principal Nursing Officer – opened a folder and glanced at the notes. "Ah, yes. Nothing I don't remember personally. Tell me, Nurse Boswell, did you enjoy midwifery?"

Anna gave her news of old colleagues who were working in the famous Edinburgh centre, and sensed a growing rapport with this woman who had taken over the top nursing job at The Princess Beatrice. Anna

9

loosened her coat and unwound the scarf, warmer than she had felt since leaving her parents' home early that morning. Matron rang for coffee and biscuits.

"I hear that the new wing is functioning now," said Anna.

Matron stirred her coffee and pushed the plate of biscuits across to Anna. "Come on, you must be starving. As I recall, that train from the West has no buffet. I know it of old. My brother lives in Taunton." She leaned back and regarded the girl, liking what she saw. A good face, serious enough to be dedicated to her work, but a tender mouth. There's compassion there without sentimentality, she thought; a good combination, and rare. "Nurse Boswell," she said, "when we have finished our coffee, I shall take you to the new block. It is true that we are gradually staffing it, but there have been many holdups with workmen, permits and snags with the sterilizing equipment. I hope to open another ward in two weeks' time when the second operating threatre comes into action."

Anna sat poised on the edge of her seat, suddenly excited. A new beginning, the best of both worlds? A new ward in her beloved training school? She drained her cup and Matron stood up, glanced at the cloudy sky and shrugged into her cloak. "If I didn't have my flowers, I would never believe that Spring is just round the corner," she said.

"It was always like this," said Anna. "And suddenly, the plane trees burst out and the magnolia in the park comes into bud." She looked up at the gaunt outlines of the bare branches. It was all a part of Beattie's. Suddenly the grey walls would brighten as the creeper came into leaf and the flowers struggled for life in the impoverished beds. They walked along the path between the buildings as it was quicker that way, although a new covered way existed to take patients and trolleys from the new block and from casualty.

She remembered the terraced garden which had been levelled to make way for the building programme. That garden had been swept away, and need never trouble her again with its memories of a man and a girl walking in the moonlight with the row of poplar trees sighing over them, and breathing a song of love. The poplars were gone, the sighing had stopped and the whine of the lift replaced the sobbing of the lonely, broken-hearted girl who had run from Dr. Rob Delaney, on the night that he had told her that he couldn't live without Carmel Medina, the dark-eyed physiotherapist who had caused a stir in the wards and medical school alike, and who had eyes for everyone, including Rob.

A girl in a white coat was carrying a radiant-heat lamp to the lift and Anna stiffened; but this girl was slight and mousey-haired, bearing no resemblance to the proud dark beauty with the curving bosom and tapering legs who had captivated the fair-haired doctor. She would be with him now, in Ireland, and if she remembered Anna at all, it would be of no importance to her that she had taken away her hope, her love and her man.

"Here we are," said Miss Joyce. The swing doors clunked softly behind them as they came into the bright ward. Delicate pastels, picked out in curtains and wall paint, mingled with the freshness of many green plants and bowls of bulbs. The ten beds were empty, the curtains separating them were swished back to the

11

walls, and the floor shone with the soft lustre of perfect cleanliness.

"It's lovely," said Anna. They inspected the clinical rooms and sluice and found everything functional and pleasing. Matron watched as Anna opened doors and cupboards, noting the good design and care that had gone into the preparation of this new unit. Another ward across the corridor was arranged in the same way, and at the end of the corridor huge double doors, half-glazed, led to the theatre. Already the gentle hum of air-conditioning pulsated, and the wide central lamp was angled over the centre of the main operating table. A separate table, resuscitator and a sophisticated incubator for an infant were in an alcove, the anaesthetic room was a dream of perfect equipment and the stillness held a promise of efficiency waiting to be set in motion.

"It's wonderful, Matron." Anna looked puzzled. "It doesn't look like a general theatre. Is it just for the two wards?"

"This is the new gynaecological block. We shall have the usual woman's ward routine and the theatre will be used only for gynae., but will include Caesarians, abortions and any complicated midwifery." She nodded towards the incubator. "Here we shall have everything we need for any emergency known to female surgery. It will cut out the possibility of cross infection in a general ward and be much more convenient in every way."

She opened the door to a pleasant side ward which contained two beds. "For isolation, or, more probably, for women who miscarry. They can rest here without having to watch other women feed their babies." She smiled sadly. "It is so cruel to leave them together. Bad

12

for the childless woman and bad for the others, when they should be feeling full of joy at the birth of their own babies. Here we shall take miscarriages, so that they are right away from the midwifery section.

Anna nodded, and as her enthusiasm rose, so her hopes of working there grew.

"We are gathering staff ready for the first patients to be admitted in ten days' time," Miss Joyce continued. "I shall appoint two junior sisters, one for each ward who will cover for theatre emergencies, and a sister in overall charge of the three units. We must have trained staff here at all times," she added firmly. "I had quite a battle with the committee who think I am staffing with too many highly qualified nurses, but I won," she said complacently and smiled. "I had some very good backing from one of the surgeons . . . quite surprising," she added, enigmatically.

"Who was that, Matron?"

"I don't know if he was here during your training: let me think. He trained at St. Thomas's and came here as house surgeon under Mr. Clarke . . . men's urological, then left two years ago to take a junior registrar's post. Now, he's Sir Horace Ritchie's second in command. Very bright young man."

Anna's hands were cold. "Who?" she said, hardly daring to think. She could recall only one man who had left two years ago, but for her there had been only one man. Her heart gave a surge of relief. Rob was a physician. Rob had never been a house surgeon; he had been on the medical heart and kidney unit. It wasn't Rob.

"Do you remember him, Nurse? Dr. Forsythe. . . . I should say Mr. Forsythe now. He has his final fellowship now."

Anna frowned. She dimly remembered a tall, thin boy walking the wards with his hands clasped behind his back. She had heard someone call him by name. Rob had stopped him one day as they walked across the garden, and she had been conscious of two very disapproving grey eyes that glanced at her and then away as if he found her either very uninteresting or quite beneath his notice. It had been as if he despised her, and when she mentioned it to Rob, he had laughed and said that any girl seen with him would have earned Slade Forsythe's deep disapproval.

It was all coming back. "Yes, I remember him," she said. How could she have forgotten the man who had been seen with Carmel Medina so often that it was said that they were on the verge of an engagement? It was hinted that Carmel was attracted to the solemn man with the craggy good looks, because he came from an old family with property and wealth rather than the possibility that she might be in love with him.

"He's with Sir Horace?" Her mind raced. The registrar on that firm would be responsible for all emergencies. If she worked on the new unit, she would have to work with Slade Forsythe, in whatever capacity she found herself. Her heart sank. First Claud knew and remembered about her and Rob, and now Mr. Forsythe! Maybe he had forgotten the small, slim girl with the pale face who went everywhere with Rob, but she knew she couldn't fool herself. He'll remember every detail, she thought. He didn't like me then and he'll be the same now! If he still smarts because Carmel rejected him, he'll probably blame me for that, she thought with unfair lack of logic.

Matron repeated her last words. "You seem to be in

14

a dream, Nurse. I asked you if you'd like to work here."
She smiled. "It *is* rather splendid," she said, taking it
for granted that Anna was slightly overwhelmed.

"I'd like it very much, Matron."

"Good, then we'll go back to my office and settle the
details. I take it that you can move in almost at once?
There are still many matters to be arranged, and you
must meet your staff before the opening."

Anna stared at her. *My staff?* "I can come back at the
weekend with my luggage, Matron. I can move in on
Saturday."

"Good! After you leave me, get measured for
uniform. I'll ask my secretary to ring the linen room."
She smiled. "You'll look very smart in green." Matron
swept away along the path outside, hurrying to avoid
the fine drizzle of rain.

"Green?" said Anna. "Green?" Even to herself she
sounded half-witted, and she was glad that Matron was
out of earshot. Green was the colour worn by sisters at
Beattie's; to go into green was the ultimate point to
reach after a stint as senior staff nurse. True, she had
her S.R.N. and S.C.M. certificates, but Beattie's had
such a high standard that she had never considered the
possibility of becoming a junior sister at such an early
age. She hurried after Matron, and the sadness, that
had lurked in the dark corners of her mind for so long,
vanished. She was back at Beattie's, she had been asked
to go into green, and she would have a brand new ward
to run. The terraced garden had gone, her wild passion
for Rob was still, crushed by the bricks of the new block,
wiped out by the work that she would do and the new
life that would rise, phoenix-like, from the ruins of the
old garden.

15

A damp spray brushed her face and she gave an involuntary shudder. The smell of rain, the touch of the cool wet evergreen on her face, told her that it was not all gone. Love such as she had for Rob would last and haunt her for ever unless she could find something to take its place. The drops on her cheek were like tears.

Shall I never be free? she thought desolately. Shall I ever forget? Rob . . . Rob . . . why did you go?

But the sorrow was something she would accept and bear, in this place where they had known such happiness. Work would take her and mould her, and in a way her loss would focus her attention on the things that really mattered in life.

Matron shook the rain from her cloak. "This is still the best protection between buildings," she said. "Make sure that Emily issues you with one of the long ones."

The old building was part of another world. Polished mahogany balustrades guarded the stairs and heavy Victorian light fittings hung over the deep stairwell beside the lift. The carpet outside Matron's office was worn and dull, awaiting the general refurbishing and clean-up of the old part. Even the smell was different. Old fashioned Ronuk floor polish made the wood block floor by the lift glow, and give a sense of manorial splendour.

"You will have a flat along there," said Matron. "I believe your sitting-room overlooks the drive." She laughed. "How times change. When I trained, there was strict segregation of the sexes! The nurses' home was like a nunnery and no male except the porters ever crossed those hallowed steps. But now, due to the increase in staff, we have been forced to let medical staff

16

use some of the trained-staff flats. I believe someone is moving into the flat across the corridor from you." She shrugged. "Not my domain. Any problems about accommodation go to Sister Manfred." She glanced at Anna's folder. "Yes . . . number six for you. Get the key when you go for your uniform."

"Thank you, Matron . . . for everything. I'll do my best to run the ward well."

"I know you will . . . but, Sister, all work and no play, you know . . . make room for personal joy." She turned away abruptly, and Anna was left outside the office again. I wonder what she meant? she thought.

Two uniform dresses fitted perfectly, and together with the rather old fashioned aprons and graceful caps that made up the exclusive Princess Beatrice uniform, Anna staggered up to her new flat to put them in drawers until she took up residence at the weekend. She fumbled in her pocket, dropping two aprons from the pile balanced on her arms, but eventually found the key. She thrust it into the keyhole and tried to turn it, but nothing happened. She glanced up at the number. Six. Funny . . . it must be the wrong key. Damn! It would mean going back for another key. Yet the tag said Six. She tried the door handle and the door opened. She pushed against it, anxious to put the slowly disintegrating bundle on to a flat surface.

Anna gasped. A pair of wet, bare arms swung her round to face the door again and an irate voice swore at her. As she landed in an untidy heap on the floor outside the room, and just before the door shut, she caught a glimpse of an angry face, flashing grey eyes and a taut, muscular body that dripped water as the naked man tried to secure a small towel round his waist.

Anna gaped and sat among the ruins of the once crisp uniform. She looked up at the door, now shut fast. She moved away from something digging into her thigh, and picked up a large screw. Once more, she looked at the number on the door. Suddenly she began to laugh as she saw the number on the flat on the opposite side of the corridor. That was six, too . . . but that six was well fixed by two large screws, unlike the one she had thought to be on her own front door.

She unlocked the other door, finding that the key fitted perfectly, and put the uniform on the bed. She smiled, a mischievous light making her eyes dance as she tapped demurely on the door from whence she had been flung so unceremoniously.

A wet, tousled head appeared and the frown deepened. Without a word, Anna thrust the long screw into his hand and she smiled up at the door number. She turned and went into her own flat and closed the door, trying to stifle the giggles that rose in her throat. Poor man, she thought.

Poor man! Not only had he attacked a strange female, but it was his fault that she had mistaken his flat for her own. After ten minutes, she peeped out. The six had been swung back and screwed into position . . . now nine, as it should have been all the time!

She picked up her bag and hurried to the stairs. She would catch the next train home and tell them her news, pack and be ready to come back on Friday, ready to start on Saturday.

She waved to Claud as she passed the lodge and he grinned. Nice girl, that, he thought. Not like some of the new ones. He thought of the last time she left the hospital, pale and tense and with eyes red with weep-

18

ing. That Dr. Delaney wasn't worth it. She was better than any of his girlfriends. Claud thought of the long line of conquests about whom Delaney boasted until Nurse Boswell came along. Funny, he'd never boasted about her, and Claud had a shrewd idea that Delaney had never managed to manoeuvre her into bed.

He stacked his invoices and slips and closed the little shutter that separated him from the outside world, and he put the kettle on to boil on the gas ring in his little room behind the lodge. The distant bell of an ambulance came nearer and Claud paused with the spoon in the paper bag of tea. The sound switched off suddenly, and he opened the shutter again to see who was driving as the vehicle, now silent, swept along the main drive which branched away from the lodge. He added another couple of teaspoonsful of tea to the already dark-brown contents of the teapot and perched a knitted cosy on the stained lid.

Five minutes later, a tap on the shutter told him that the ambulance driver was ready for a cuppa, and Claud opened the door to admit him to the shambles that surrounded the porter during the working hours.

"What we got then?" Claud liked to know even the most trivial details about staff and patients alike.

"A fracture for Faraday Ward . . . silly blighter trod on a ladder rung that wasn't there."

"Femur?" Claud asked knowledgeably.

The ambulance man took a bite from a badly squashed bun that Claud offered to him. "Never learn, do they?" he said, his mouth spilling dry crumbs. They discussed the number of cases admitted that day, and Claud listened with avid attention. It was a secret sorrow that he couldn't be in two places at once. True,

19

he could see most of what went on, the comings and goings of staff and some of the patients, but it would be wonderful to be there when the ambulances were unloaded, to see the suffering relatives and to savour the full drama of the casualty department. He handed another bun to the man, but far from having the effect he wanted, that was, making the man more relaxed and ready to talk, it shut him up completely until he had downed another cup of strong, sweet tea.

"New unit opens next week or thereabouts," said Claud, and the man grunted. "Does that come into your run?"

The ambulance man gulped.

"I heard they were having another fleet of small cars for emergencies that can get themselves into an ambulance," Claud persisted.

"Yes, but not for the new lot." He stirred the tea leaves in the bottom of the cup, and Claud hastily added a watered-down but fresh supply of tea. "They'll need us experienced men for that one. It has been known for some of us to deliver babies before they get into hospital," he said loftily. Claud sighed inwardly, resigning himself to hearing for the hundredth time the story of the one occasion when this had happened to his guest. He allowed his attention to wander while the man droned on, certain now that nothing of interest had happed in casualty during the day.

Claud cleared away the cups and locked the cupboard that contained all his treasured on-duty possessions, like the teapot and supplies of tea, milk and sugar. The man took the hint, looked at his watch and agreed that it was time to "pack it in". He left Claud to bolt the shutter from the inside before switching the telephone over to the main entrance for the night. Claud heard the swish of wheels as the ambulance went slowly past to the depot, to be tidied and checked so that it was ready for the next call. Princess Beatrice Hospital had her own small fleet of vehicles, and thanks to the foresight of the Victorians who planned on a grand scale, there was plenty of space for garages, turning points, service areas and room for further expansion of the hospital in an area of London that was over-crowded, stifling in its concentration of roads, narrow lanes and masses of people living in the old houses and brash modern flats behind the park.

The rain had stopped, and for the first time for a week traces of blue sky, fast becoming dark, edged between the banks of lazy cloud. Claud buttoned his donkey-jacket and pulled the woollen hat down over his ears, ready for the ten-minute walk to his home. A sports car stopped by the lodge.

"Too late, mate," said Claud, "I'm off duty, ain't I?" He stood in the doorway of the lodge, however, unable to resist waiting long enough to see who was behind the wheel, but ready to tell him to go to the main lodge if he wanted Claud to telephone someone within the hospital.

He grinned. It was only the man from the flower shop, the smart shop that did overseas orders and the like. Looked a regular fancy-boy, but even Claud had to admit that Michael Johns knew his job, delivered fresh, well-presented flowers and was rapidly building up a lucrative business. He waved cheerfully to the porter. "Who's that for?" said Claud.

"No name . . . never had one like this."

"What ward?"

"Not a ward, a number in the nurses' home." Claud

went over to the car and looked down at the sheaf of roses wrapped in plastic film.

" 'ello, 'ello!" he said respectfully. "Wonder who it is?"

"You mean you don't know? Claud, you disappoint me. I thought you knew everyone in this hospital." Michael grinned, knowing the man's reputation for curiosity. "I thought you *must* know, Claud. Trouble is, I've got two wreaths to deliver and I've a date tonight." His ingenuous face gave nothing away.

"Well, I suppose I could take them. By rights, you ought to go to the other lodge . . . but these ought to be in water and *they* wouldn't bother," said Claud, self-righteously. "I'm off duty, but I'll take them." He put out a hand. "Any card with them?" he asked hopefully.

"No. I was out when they were ordered. Paid cash and was very sure of the room number, but no card, no name."

Claud felt a prickle of excitement. One of the nurses with an unknown admirer? It happened often enough, but not to the tune of out-of-season roses flown in from foreign parts.

"Take care of them . . . if there's nobody there, could you put them in a bucket of water? They will last for a couple of weeks in the cool," said Michael, then thrust the huge bouquet into the man's arms and gave him a wicked smile. "Do tell when I come next. I could do with more orders like that one."

Claud was left feeling faintly ridiculous, holding the roses. He walked to the entrance to the nurses' home and glanced up at the windows. They all seemed empty and blank, but there must be someone there. He went into the lobby and looked up at the wooden board with the sliding covers to indicate who was in and who was out. Most of the spaces had hand-written names on peel-off rectangles of paper. There were two blanks and one of them was number six, the room number on the flowers. He read the names. The empty slots must be for new arrivals. The Home Sister brushed him aside. "What are you doing here, Claud?"

She stuck a name to number nine. Dr. Slade Forsythe. There was one slot empty now. He told the sister that the flowers were for number six. She glanced at him sharply. "Are you sure?"

He showed her the small, decorated label. 'Number Six, Nurses' Home, St. Beatrice.' "Shall I take them up, Sister?" he said hopefully.

"No." She looked absent-minded, as if remembering something. "Sister Boswell will not be here for two days; I'll see to them." She seemed to realise that he was staring at her. "Someone wanted to welcome her back, I expect." She touched the longest of the roses which peeped through the edge of the wrapping. "How beautiful they are! I'll put them in water. She'll be pleased to see them arranged when she moves in." She didn't move. "Who brought them, Claud?"

"Mr. Johns from the shop, Sister, but he didn't know who ordered them. I asked," he added, as if Sister would never have suspected him of such initiative.

Sister unwrapped the plastic and loosened the surrounding fronds of delicate fern that accompanied the roses. "I have just the vase for them," she said. "With the heating turned down in her room, they will be perfect when she comes on Friday night."

Sister walked away along the corridor, turning the flowers from side to side. They were perfect, and she

23

knew that the fact that she did not know who had sent them would niggle in the back of her mind all the evening. No card, no indication of any kind, and the sender couldn't have known that the new sister wouldn't be living in until Friday. There wasn't anything to say that the flowers had been ordered by telephone, as many of the bouquets for patients were ordered. Agents of such firms usually had their names on the wrappings but the film was plain and clear and only Michael's shop address was on the printed ribbon.

The porter walked across the park and looked back at the hospital. It was easy to make out the fan-shaped architecture of the old building and he glanced at it with unconscious affection. Good old Beattie's. So much of his life had been tied up with her. Like so many local people, he had been in and out of the place since he was a baby, first with feeding difficulties, then with a broken leg when he fell out of a tree in the park. There had been plenty of other hazards, too, like having a bead removed from his nose and a bad boil that needed lancing under anaesthetic. Beattie's was a solid, efficient friend and he had a certain pride in working there.

A mate from the psychiatric hospital, who worked in the kitchens, made room for him in the pub. Claud regaled him with details of an accident case he had seen in casualty while they drank halves of bitter and ate a couple of pork pies. There was plenty to watch, as several hospital workers used the pub across the park and nurses went there with boyfriends. Two junior house surgeons, looking pale and overworked, recognised Claud and nodded, establishing him with his friend as someone well-known at the hospital. They bought refills and settled down to a satisfactory evening.

The pub filled with local people and more doctors from both hospitals. Some went through to the dining-room and Claud noticed that Michael Johns went through with a dazzling blonde girl in a very tight and well-filled blouse. Claud started on his third drink and made a mental note that Johns was no fancy-boy after all.

Out of the crowd waiting to be served came a man with vivid blue eyes. With his looks and stature and an air of confidence and authority which came with the knowledge that personal charm will gain entry to places where lesser mortals might not dare to go, he dominated every other man at the bar. A slight weakness in the chin under the self-indulgent mouth only added to the man's good looks, and a seat became miraculously vacant for him as soon as he looked for a place. People glanced at him curiously, and the man with Claud said, "Wasn't he at Beattie's?"

Claud nodded. He pictured the buttoned-up expression that Nurse Boswell had had when he had mentioned Dr. Delaney. He'd told her that he was in Ireland . . . well, he had gone there two years ago. She hadn't kept in touch, that was certain. He wondered if she still went starry-eyed over him, or if she had another boyfriend. She was a really nice girl . . . too good for him.

Claud buried his nose in his glass, determined not to be spotted by that cynical, roving eye. So it must have been him . . . *he* sent the roses. It was as plain as the nose on his face. Dr. Delaney was back in town, and he had sent the roses.

"Poor little gal," he muttered. "I wonder when she'll find out he's back?"

CHAPTER TWO

SIR HORACE RITCHIE beamed. He turned to Matron, and to the young nurses it looked as if he would embrace their august chief nursing officer, but instead he followed her into the surgeons' room, where a discreet celebration of sherry and an indeterminate but vaguely birthday-cake edifice was cut and the pieces handed round to celebrate the opening of the new unit. One or two camera-bulbs flashed and the local reporter hastily drank his sherry and rushed off to catch the late edition of the local evening paper.

Anna eased the unfamiliar and stiff tape which was rubbing her chin where the lacy bow of junior Ward Sister gave evidence of her promotion. It was a proud moment for all concerned, and for Sir Horace, a climax to a lifetime spent in the interests of his patients. His thinning hair, grey at the temples, and his deeply lined forehead, only added to his dignity and not a single person in the room thought of him as nearing retirement age and so coming to the end of his hospital career. But his contentment was mixed with the secret knowledge that soon he would ease up, and let younger, stronger and perhaps, he mused, if he were honest, fresher men with progressive ideas and more to offer modern surgery, take his place and carry on the worthy traditions of Princess Beatrice Hospital.

Anna was conscious of someone looking at her and was in time to see Slade Forsythe look away. She felt herself blushing, not because his glance held any flattering approval or that she reacted in any way to his scrutiny, but she now knew who it was who lived in room number nine in the same corridor of the nurses' home. During the opening ceremony, they had not come into any close proximity, and Anna hoped that it would be so for as long as possible. She knew that when the wards grew full and busy, she would have to talk to him, ask him about patients and be told of their treatments, but today was an artificial day, with patients sitting up in bed who were in for minor complaints, or operations that were not emergencies. As Matron said, there must be patients but it would hardly do for one of them to be acutely ill while Sir Horace and his wife cut the white ribbon at the doorway to the theatre!

Sir Horace was holding out his hand. "My dear Sister," he said, "how good to see you again. It does my heart good to see former students returning to Beattie's." He smiled. "And you look very well in green, my dear." He turned to his wife. "We must arrange a dinner, darling. This time we have two new sisters to celebrate. It's time we had another party."

Lady Ritchie smiled at Matron, who exchanged a glance with her as if to say, 'We have done this so often, but he does love his little parties, doesn't he?'

Anna glanced round the room and saw that Slade Forsythe had left without a word to anyone. She felt oddly disappointed. She didn't want to meet him and talk to him, but somehow, now that he had left, ignoring her, it gave him an advantage. She recalled how he had looked at her, solemnly and without expression, just as he had done two years ago when she was the constant companion of Rob Delaney.

If he was as bad-tempered as this on a social occasion, what would he be like to work with? she thought resentfully. What did it matter if he thought she was a frivolous girl who didn't pick very reliable boyfriends? He hadn't exactly been lucky when he went out with Carmel, so he had no reason to look down his aristocratic nose at her!

She was uncomfortable, however, remembering his face when she gave him the metal screw which had fallen from the door of his room. She had embarrassed him, not knowing who he was, and it was bound to rankle with him.

Ah, well, she was off duty for the afternoon, going off late and returning just to take report and to check the late drugs before the night staff came on. Sister Susan Johnston, who was in charge of the other ward, would be on duty and there was nothing to do that couldn't wait until the morning. Anna wandered down to the garden and breathed the fresh air. The incinerator was not working and the first warmth of Spring made the dark earth look alive. She felt for the letters in her pocket and wondered if Claud had any stamps.

At the lodge she paused and tapped on the shutter. A strong whiff of cigarette smoke came out of the half-open window and Claud appeared. He brightened. "Any stamps, Claud?" she said.

"How many d'you want? Nice to see you back, *Sister*. You look real classy in green." He grinned. "Get the flowers? All right, were they? I took them over myself; couldn't have that lot in Casualty messing them about. Sister took them from me. I hope she did them right. Mr. Johns said they needed plenty of water."

"They are perfectly lovely." She hesitated. "If Michael brought them, didn't he give you a card?"

"You don't know who sent them, Sister?" Claud

28

looked blank, as he did when he knew something but wasn't sure if he ought to talk about it.

"I haven't had time to check. I came in late last night and there was only time to put out uniform for today, have a bath and get to bed. It was a lovely welcome to find the flowers. I must ring my parents . . . but they would have sent a message, and roses out of season are not their idea of necessary expense." Anna laughed. "Perhaps it was Sir Horace. He's such a dear and he has been known to make extravagant gestures . . . but there again, he would have sent a card or at least have hinted that he'd sent them when I saw him at the opening ceremony." She began to be really puzzled.

"You've got a secret admirer, that's what, Sister."

"What rubbish! Apart from the nursing staff and Sir Horace – and now they've seen me, the rest of the hospital! – nobody knows I'm here." She frowned. "You don't think that Michael Johns thought I'd be intrigued and show them to everyone? It might be his way of drumming up more trade."

"No, it wasn't him," Claud said quickly.

"Claud! You know something. Come on, tell me."

He looked very unhappy. "I don't know nothing."

"You do. I've seen that expression too often, Claud. You might as well give; you know you'll never keep it to yourself."

"You aren't going to like it, Sister."

"You mean there's a dark and horrible stranger who has designs on me? I don't believe you." She laughed, but his slightly desperate look made her serious. "Tell me, Claud," she said gently. "Whoever it was, I can't blame you for it, can I?"

"I went to the new boozer the night they came," he

admitted miserably. "There were a lot of people from Beattie's there."

"I imagine there would be," she said dryly. "I might go there myself, soon."

"There was someone there I haven't seen for a very long time, and I heard he'd been hanging round the hospital earlier in the day."

A sensation of impending disaster made Anna clench her hands on the edges of her cloak. "Who?" she whispered.

"Dr. Bloody Delaney," he said, and turned away to get some stamps.

"No . . . no! It isn't true. You said he was in Ireland." Bright spots of colour appeared in her cheeks, and her eyes clouded with tears. "No, Claud. It's wicked to say such things when you know it isn't true."

But she knew he spoke the truth, and she knew that Rob had heard that she was back at the hospital. Why now? Why come back just when she had plucked up enough courage to return to the place that held so many memories? She could almost hear the gentle sound of the poplars in a breeze, smell the syringa that had bloomed in the terraced garden, and feel the pressure of his arms about her.

"You all right, Sister?"

Anna shook herself and smiled weakly. "I'm fine. Thank you for telling me, Claud. It wasn't easy for you, I know." She turned away.

"You forgot your stamps!" he called, but she did not hear. Anger took the place of her trembling weakness. How *dare* he? How dared Rob come back and take it for granted that all he had to do was to send her flowers, and she would collapse into his arms as if the two years had never been? She quickened her steps and ran up the stairs to her room, unlocked the door and flung it wide.

The roses were gracefully arranged in a copper bowl and the fronds of fern made a hazy backcloth of pale green. Anna paused, struck by their beauty and, loving flowers as she did, she could hardly bring herself to do what she had to do. She took the lovely blooms and thrust them into her waste basket.

The cleaner might take them out and put them back into the vase if she left them there. Anna put the bin outside the door, deciding to change and to take them down to the dustbin. She unpinned her cap with weary fingers, and the door closed softly. Suddenly she was very tired. She lay on the bed and tried to relax, but her anger had made her tense and unable to lie still. "I'll take them now," she said to herself, slipped her shoes back on her feet and patted her hair.

The door across the corridor was open, and she saw the back view of Slade Forsythe. He closed the door without seeing her, and she could have sworn that in one hand he held a rose.

She tipped the roses into the bin and went back to her room. She tried to read, then decided to go down early for a meal before checking with the ward. She chatted with the three other sisters in the small dining-room and was made to feel welcome. Her disquiet began to go, the comfort and friendliness acting like a balm to her bruised spirit, and when she left to go back to the ward she was almost back to normal.

Rob can't be on the staff, she thought. The others would have mentioned it as he was always popular with women and such a handsome man would raise some comment. She breathed more easily. Just passing

31

through. It might have been a peace offering, left on an impulse before he returned to his life of domesticity with Carmel in Ireland.

She smiled. The thought of Rob with a wife and children was ludicrous . . . but hadn't she dreamed of just that for herself and Rob?

A lift whined and a theatre trolley met her in the corridor. She quickened her steps. Lights shone in the new theatre and a bag of soiled linen lay by the lift. She peeped through the glass panel of the door and saw that the theatre staff were clearing after a case. There was no need to dress up, so she went in to find out what was happening. From the surgeons' room came masculine voices, laughing. Anna smiled. That was a good sign. If a case went well, there was always an air of elation and relief and the surgon was usually good-humoured. She wondered who had done the operation, and Susan Johnston came to meet her.

"What's happened?" said Anna, taking off her cuffs and rolling up her sleeves.

"No need for you to get messed up," said Susan. "All done and everything under control. They just have the floor to swab, and the instruments are in the steriliser. You can dry them and put them away if you like, while I check my ward."

Anna glanced into the incubator where a red-faced infant screwed up his face and whimpered. The waxy remains of the vernix caseosa that often covers the newly born lay in the folds of flesh of the elbows and neck. He gave a mournful howl, and his colour became more normal. Anna smiled.

"Caesarian," said Susan, stating the obvious. "Nice baby, but he was beginning to complain, so Sir Horace

32

decided to bring the mother here. She lost the last one, so he was doubly anxious, bless him." She went away, untying her theatre gown as she went.

"Do you make a point of arriving when all the work is done?"

Anna turned, smiling, thinking that Sir Horace was teasing her. The smile faded as she looked up into the cold grey eyes of Slade Forsythe, who was certainly not teasing.

"What do you mean?" Anna stared at him, horrified by the controlled anger in his voice and face. It wasn't the anger of a man who had needed extra help and been denied it by a thoughtless woman. This went deeper, and it struck a chill in her heart. His words lashed her and she knew he was deliberately trying to make her suffer. But she wasn't the only one who was suffering, she realised. Behind the cold anger was sadness . . . a deep and agonising sadness, and her own reaction was cooled by his suffering.

"I didn't know there was a Caesar," she said, quietly. "Sister Johnston was in charge, and it certainly wouldn't have helped her if I'd barged in and tried to take over."

Her cool brittle voice got through to him. He put a hand over his eyes and looked suddenly very tired. "I'm sorry," he said stiffly, "that was unforgivable." He wiped his face with the towel draped round his neck and the muscles on his broad shoulders glistened with sweat. "I must get a shower," he said, abruptly, and went into the surgeons' room.

Anna watched him go and found that her hand had reached out as if to touch him, to make him stay. She wanted to tell him that whatever it was that made him suffer excused his manner . . . Her hand itched to smooth the dark hair away from the damp brow, as one would soothe a child.

I must be clean round the bend, she thought. He's a very unpleasant man. But she knew that the look in his eyes would haunt her, and she had an uneasy feeling that somehow she was the cause of it.

She polished the hot instruments and laid them back in the glass-fronted cupboard. She checked the packs of drip sets and dressings so that everything was ready at a moment's notice if the theatre was needed for an emergency, and remembered the words of her first theatre sister.

"Remember, Nurse: No theatre is ever clear. It is ready, not cleared. You must take it for granted that in five minutes, another trolley will come through that doorway with a very ill patient. We must have everything ready even if it means hours of boring, repetitive work, making sure that everything is working and every drug is up to date and accessible. Each piece of equipment must be serviced as soon as it is unusable, all emergency batteries checked after each case, and every instrument oiled and clean ready for sterilisation."

Anna had thought her fussy and over-officious, but now her own experienced eye took in details missed by the nurses clearing the operating room, and when the floor gleamed damply and the trolleys sat neatly in their places once more, it was as if she had been working there for ages. Added familiarity made the department more completely hers, and when Susan came back, in green again with her bow tilted slightly under her chin, they surveyed their little domain with pride and pleasure.

"This is going to be a good place," said Susan. "Some are, some aren't . . . but I can feel it. Funny, a kind of atmosphere comes out of the walls that tells you at once. I knew it at the opening and now we've been blooded, so to speak . . . oh, what am I saying?" She giggled. "Well, you know what I mean."

"I feel it too," said Anna. "If only. . . ."

"What? Doubts already?"

"No, not about the unit, but how do you think Mr. Forsythe will fit in? I've never seen him operate, but I assume that I shall have that pleasure quite soon, unless I manage to leave it all to you."

Susan raised an eyebrow at the edge in Anna's voice.

"Slade Forsythe? Are you serious? He's great in the theatre."

"I didn't mean his work. He must be O.K. as far as work goes or he wouldn't have his present position," she said, almost to herself.

"But he's nice! He's dish of the month as far as most of the female staff are concerned. Surely those shoulders and that good strong manly profile didn't escape your notice completely, or are you still. . . . ?" Susan bit her lip. "Sorry, that was stupid of me."

Anna shrugged and bent to pick up a glove packet that had been left on a stool. "You know that Rob Delaney came back?" Susan asked bluntly.

"I heard," said Anna.

"He was asking about you." Susan looked uncomfortable.

"I wasn't there, but I heard about it. Of course, he would have to run into Sister Martin, who has been here since the year dot and never, but never, forgets a bit of gossip."

"Oh, my godfathers! Not *her* still here?"

"Afraid so. She told him you were coming back to work here before you knew yourself, most likely. She's in cahoots with Sister Admin., and doesn't miss anything." Susan's candid eyes viewed her with interest. "I wasn't here when you left, but you know how gossip gets round. Like to tell me a bit about yourself? In this hotbed of gossip, it's as well to keep the record straight."

"I suppose Claud told you something?" enquired Anna.

"No. That's a strange thing. Claud sings your praises and shuts up anyone who tries to find out if you still see the glamorous Dr. Delaney."

The theatre faded into darkness as they left and the one light over the steriliser glowed softly through the glass door. Susan followed Anna into her office, glanced at the clock and said she would come back after Anna had given the report to the night staff. "I'll look in on the Caesar and settle her, and we can walk over together," she said.

The ward was quiet and the two young sisters followed the trolley carrying the new baby as far as the lift. He was now a bright pink and sucked his fist hungrily. "He'll do very well," said Anna. "I expect his mother will be glad to have him back in maternity with her."

"I went over and she's asleep. She'll have a pleasant surprise to wake up and find her son and heir in the nursery near her, none the worse for his entry into the world." Susan sighed. "If I didn't have a boyfriend at home, I'd fall for Mr. Forsythe."

"He didn't impress me much," Anna said shortly. "In fact each time I've seen him so far, he's been very offhand, and when he saw me come into the theatre I thought he was angry enough to hit me!"

"But he's a lovely man," said Susan in an exaggerated Irish accent. "A lovely man . . . a broth of a boy."

Anna laughed. "You could have fooled me!"

Susan looked dreamy. "Quite a sight, our Mr. Forsythe, holding that tiny scrap of humanity in his strong, brown hands, making it breathe. It's funny how touching it is to see a really powerful man being very very gentle with a baby or a young animal. Fair turned me old heart over, it did."

"Coming up to my room for coffee?" said Anna.

"Better still, let's try the new pub. I haven't had the courage to go alone, and I hear it's very good. We can leave a message with the main lodge in case I'm needed. I'm on call tonight, I believe. We can get back in under five minutes; very handy arrangement. We shall probably become hardened drinkers if we wait there for emergencies."

A reluctant moon shone through the dark treetops in the park as they skirted the edge and walked into the driveway of the Golden Falcon. It was a mixture of local pub, with an ordinary bar for those who did not care for the smarter, club-like atmosphere of the lounge, a snack counter with good bar food, and a well-decorated and discreetly lit restaurant. Each department was well patronised and the girls strolled about, exploring, before settling at the snack counter with soft drinks and chicken sandwiches.

"I'm starving," said Susan. "The Caesar came in just as I was going for supper so I haven't eaten. Sister from the general theatre rang and offered to take the case in the main theatre, but I thought we might as well dive in the deep end." She sipped her Coke. "I think it will work very well. Even though Sister Baxter is in charge of all theatres, she hasn't interfered today. She rang to check that all was well and told me where she would be if I wanted to contact her, but it's good to know she has confidence in us."

"So, it's you and I with the occasional visit from the departmental theatre sister? Nice . . . I couldn't ask for a better arrangement."

"Except for Mr. Forsythe?" Susan smiled mischievously.

"I'll eat him for breakfast if he's rude again," said Anna, with more vehemence than she realised.

"My, my, he has upset you! I can't think why."

"I've yet to see him smile, he looks at me as if I was dragged in by the cat and left on the mat, and he has a nasty temper." Anna told Susan about her meeting with him when she mistook his room for her own. "I've never seen anyone so furious. He had wet hair dripping over his face and I didn't recognise him until afterwards. Well, would you expect your surgical registrar to appear stark naked and bundle you out of his room?"

The memory was suddenly very funny and Anna began to giggle. Susan imagined the scene, and soon they were helplessly laughing. "Don't tell me any more . . . I shall burst out laughing in the ward when he comes in, if I'm not careful," gasped Susan. "But I think you misjudge him. He's shy, that's all."

"Shy?" The one word held all the disbelief and annoyance that, even when she could laugh, came through to irritate her. "He's not shy. He's the most supercilious, self-righteous, boring man I know."

"And he's just come in," said Susan, softly. She grinned. "Shall I wave? Shall I call him over?"

"Only if you want a quiet tête-à-tête with him," said Anna sweetly. "If you ask him here I shall be out of that door like a scalded cat! I've seen him once . . . twice, today, and that's plenty."

"It's all right. Panic over. He's joined two of the men from the hospital and they've gone in to eat. Come to think of it, he must have missed dinner, too. So even the gods have to eat!" Susan ordered more food. "I shall end up by spending more than if we'd gone in for a full meal in the restaurant," she said.

Anna was content to sit and watch the people coming and going. It was almost like the hospital, she thought. In this place there was a cross-section of all the life in the local community, just as there was in the busy hospital. There were the doctors and young surgeons in the restaurant, with many of the local businessmen and their wives or girlfriends, a mixture of youngsters round the jukebox in the outer coffee bar who could have come from any background at all. They wore a uniform of the latest in jeans and shoes, and from their appearance it could not be known if they were sons and daughters of the bank manager or the window cleaner. Here, as in Outpatients, everyone was just another human being, classless and an essential part of the whole community.

"Michael's looking very smart tonight," said Susan. The florist waved and came over to the two empty seats by the girls. "Hello," said Susan.

"Mind if we sit here? The other lounge is jam-packed," said Michael. Anna smiled. The girl with him wasn't the gorgeous blonde he had steered so tenderly

39

into the restaurant the other evening; at least, she assumed that it was a different girl. Even Claud couldn't have fabricated such a description to fit this rather pleasant, ordinary little girl who obviously wasn't getting the full treatment of wining and dining that Claud had so colourfully portrayed. This one had to make do with a sandwich and half a pint of bitter!

"Working late," said Michael. "Tessa stayed on and we've finished a rush order, so the least I could do was to feed the woman."

"You work in the shop?" said Anna.

"Mostly behind the scenes. I make up the bouquets and wreaths."

"So you wouldn't know who ordered flowers?"

"There's usually a card . . . except for the roses the other day. He was very fussy: wouldn't leave a name, and Michael had to go to Covent Garden specially for the flowers."

"Did you see him?" said Anna, knowing in her heart that Rob had been the man. She was deeply disturbed. It wasn't like Rob to go to any trouble unless there was something for him to be gained by . . . a gift, by flattery, by so carefully selecting expensive roses.

Susan was talking to Michael of other things, but Anna knew that she had not seen the last of Rob and she wondered if she would have the strength to resist him if he came back into her life. She tried to think of Carmel, but somehow, the dark sensual face wouldn't come into mental focus. Would Carmel love a man enough to wash his clothes, cook his meals and make a home for a busy doctor? The more she thought about it, the more unlikely it seemed and when the girls walked back to the hospital, Anna was very quiet.

'He's come back for me,' she thought, 'and I was stupid to think he would ever let a girl go without possessing her, completely.' The fact that she had refused to go away with him, to sleep with him and eventually to take a flat with him had made him very determined to make her come to him.

It might have been her refusal, a situation which he found a slight to his ego and a sauce to his anticipation of her surrender, that had made him first turn to Carmel in an attempt to make Anna jealous. But he hadn't taken into account the fact that Carmel was passionate and free with her favours, eager to add his scalp to her collection as the best looking man at Beattie's. He had succumbed to her completely, and had convinced himself that Anna was not to be compared with the woman who held nothing back and seemed to adore him.

From her room, Anna heard Slade Forsythe unlock his door and there was silence. She turned over in bed and tried to empty her mind of Rob, of the excitement of her first day as a sister and of the fact that Slade Forsythe had the power to make her want him to think well of her . . . only professionally, of course, she told herself . . . not as a person. The last conscious thought was of roses . . . no, not roses, only one rose, as deeply red as her heart's blood, held in the firm hand of a stern-looking man.

The alarm woke her and she shut off the sound, aware that sleep had not refreshed her mind. Uneasy dreams had haunted her and she hurried through her dressing, pinning her mind down to the day ahead and the routine she had decided to start in her new ward as fresh admissions came in. Susan had the morning off, and Anna popped briskly into her ward to make sure that the day staff nurse had arrived and that everything was under control before going to her own small office.

In spite of her sombre thoughts concerning Rob, she couldn't help feeling proud and elated at her new status. She rolled up her sleeves neatly and pulled the frilled cuffs over the edges. It was a relic of the old days but traditional and very attractive, although many members of the hospital committee had tried to substitute modern uniforms of ill-fitting sack-like dresses with no aprons for the gracefully gathered cotton dresses with well-cut aprons which were, in fact, changed more frequently than many of the modern uniforms, and were hygienic as well as good to look at. The caps of the nurses in training had been brought up to date and perched on the backs of the heads of the student nurses like small greaseproof paper envelopes, but the caps worn by staff nurses, junior sisters and departmental sisters were exactly as the caps had been when Florence Nightingale walked the wards at Scutari. In fact she had come back to advise the equipping of the Princess Beatrice Hospital at its inception.

Sir Horace made his round with his new house surgeon, an eager young man who had a tendency to drop the notes whenever Sir Horace asked him a question. It was strange to think he could be frightened of the great man. Anna had never formed the impression that Sir Horace could be other than charming and easy-going, but today, she watched him objectively; seeing him in his capacity as senior consultant for the first time. During her training, she had not worked on his wards and knew nothing of the keen mind and surprisingly caustic tongue that he possessed and used on occasion.

Perhaps that's why Slade Forsythe is so unpleasant, she thought, but surely he doesn't possess a lighter side to his nature? He's sarcastic and overbearing all the time. But she remembered Susan's words, 'A lovely man, a broth of a boy,' and wondered who was right.

Anna took the bundle of notes from Dr. Smith's nerveless hands before he could drop them again. Sir Horace glanced at her with a twinkle in his eyes and she shook her head at him. He was amused to see that she knew his bark was the only fierce thing about him, and became more reasonable towards his house surgeon. After the ward round, he dismissed him and Anna served coffee in her office while Sir Horace stretched out his legs as he sat deep in the leather chair.

"You must come out to dinner with us, my dear. Do it for all the new sisters, you know." He gave a wicked grin. "I have to show my wife the opposition. Keeps her on her toes, you know, to see what pretty women work with me."

Anna smiled. "I think you do it to convince her that the tales about you aren't true." He looked amazed. "I think she hears rumours that you are a tyrant who bullies his staff and it's your way of showing her that some people are *not* frightened of you," said Anna.

He laughed. "You certainly aren't . . . and that young man will soon lick into shape. I only do it to make them see that this is a serious business." He dunked a ginger biscuit in his coffee. "Can I have coffee with you every day? I don't get ginger biscuits at home," he added plaintively. "My wife says I'm putting on weight."

He took out a diary. "When are you off duty? We can have a meal at the new place. I hear the food is passable and we would be available for anything that crops up here."

She told him about her off-duty rota and he made a note. "I'll check with the others. I like to make it a real party." He winked. "If I invite Matron, she invites us back to that very pleasant flat afterwards for coffee, and she makes very good coffee."

"There's really no need," began Anna, but she saw that the arrangement would give him a great deal of pleasure so she smiled and thanked him. "Best bib and tucker?" she said.

"Why not? What a good idea. We can have the private room and make it a real party. I like to see you all in pretty clothes. Often wonder if I'd had a daughter...." He stood up and frowned. "You have no right to keep me here talking, Sister. I have calls to make."

He was gone and Anna thought how sad it was that the man who solved so many problems for others, giving women healthy children through his skill and care, and saving the lives of mothers and babies, should have no children of his own. She took round the ten o'clock drugs and wrote up her notes on the new admissions, two new patients who were very different from the women who had sat up in bed like film extras while the new unit was opened.

One girl was pale and nervous. Undernourished, thought Anna, and a quick examination of her eyelids showed a very anaemic mucosa. Anna made a note to make sure the house surgeon wrote her up for blood tests. From her history, it was clear that she had lost a lot of blood over a period of several months and it was

44

suspected that she had uterine fibroids, a collection of hard but innocent growths in her womb that bled and gave rise to all kinds of unpleasant symptoms but could be removed safely.

Anna explained what would happen to her from the time of the injection which would make her drowsy to the time when she would be back again from the operating theatre, not necessarily feeling sick.

"But I thought everyone was very sick and it hurt the stitches," Sandra Bowen said. "I was dreading it more than anything."

"You may be sick. I can't guarantee that you won't feel nauseated, but I do know that anaesthetics are so good now that unless you are in the theatre a very long time and the anaesthetist isn't as good as he might be, you will wake up easily and be relaxed," replied Anna. She could feel the woman relaxing as she explained, and was glad that her early training at Beattie's had stressed the importance of telling patients as much as possible about their conditions to gain their confidence and full co-operation.

"You will be here, Sister?" said Sandra, with a sudden look of panic.

"I shall be on duty all tomorrow afternoon and evening. I shall see you into the anaesthetic room and be here when you return. Sister Johnston will help Sir Horace or Mr. Forsythe, and you will be back before you know you've been anaesthetised."

"Oh, Sister! Will that nice young doctor do me? I'd like that ever so much."

"You will be asleep, so it shouldn't matter to you," smiled Anna.

"He was so kind to me when I first came to Outpatients, Sister. He asked about my family and how they would manage while I was in here. Do you know, he gave me a letter to apply for a stay in a convalescent home . . . not just me, my husband's coming, and my mother is going to look after Benny . . . he's my little boy. It will be like a real holiday. I think Mr. Forsythe is wonderful."

Anna patted her hand and went on to the next patient. By the end of the round, she was frowning. Everyone she spoke to made a point of praising the saturnine, bad-tempered man who had been so rude to her. It must be me, she thought, miserably. He doesn't like me for some reason and I'm the only one he treats like this.

She sat and chewed the end of her pen and gazed out of the window. Across the ambulance park strode two figures. Anna stood by the window and watched the house surgeon and the surgical registrar in deep conversation. The younger man said something and grinned, and Slade Forsythe threw back his head and laughed. The perfect white teeth showed in a wide smile, the grey eyes almost disappeared and his whole body shook with amusement. Anna felt herself smiling just to see him like that. He *could* laugh . . . he could look human, but not for her.

CHAPTER THREE

ANNA put down the house phone and smiled. Sir Horace had rung Matron, and the party was arranged. A small private party would be gathering in the side room at the Falcon to celebrate the opening of the unit, and to greet the two young new sisters. He really was rather sweet, thought Anna. There was no sense of urgency in the ward, and the few surgical cases from the day before were progressing well with no complications. Slade Forsythe had looked in briefly and gone round the ward in record time, hurrying on to Susan Johnston's ward.

"Everything seems all right here, Sister," Mr. Forsythe had said crisply. "If you need me, have me bleeped, but I must go to the other side; Mrs. Morris isn't very well."

"The salpingectomy yesterday?"

He looked surprised. "Yes . . . have you seen her?"

"I went along yesterday when Sister Johnston was off duty, as the staff nurse was worried. I thought it right that she should send for you rather than the house surgeon."

"Quite right. I ordered treatment and it wasn't enough," he accepted the responsibility coolly, "so it blew up into a bad infection and had to come out. Just as well we got her into the theatre before the day staff left."

Anna nodded. Once more, she had been on ward duty and not on call for the theatre when Mr. Forsythe had operated. Susan Johnston had scrubbed up with two medical students while Anna settled the patients in both of the small wards. He looked at her as if wanting to say more, but picked up his notes and left quickly without another word.

I wonder if he will go to the party? thought Anna. Or if he is too unsociable to join his staff for dinner?

Sandra Bowen called as Anna went into the ward. "Sister . . . thank you for being here yesterday." Anna remembered telling Sandra that she would be on duty when she came back from the operating theatre after having her uterine fibroids removed. Anna beckoned a student nurse. "When I woke up and you were over there, sitting at your desk, I knew everything would be all right, Sister."

"How do you feel now, Sandra?" She helped the nurse to raise the young woman from the crumpled pillows and gently put Sandra's arms round the shoulders of the nurse. Deftly, Anna made the bed comfortable and arranged the pillows so that the patient sank back gratefully into a nest of softness which still supported her in a sitting position. "You must do your exercises, you know, even if it is uncomfortable. The sooner you are well, the sooner you can go for convalescence, you know."

Sandra was very pale but after two pints of blood transfused in the theatre and another two bottles during the night, she was better, and the drip canula could now be removed from the vein in her arm. As Anna strapped a small dressing over the puncture wound, Sandra smiled.

"Better?" said Anna.

"Better, Sister . . . you've no idea. I feel blooming uncomfortable, but it's nothing. It's been done, and I can look forward to a future again."

"A future? But you had a future even if you didn't have the operation."

Sandra shook her head. The very new bedjacket, brought in by her husband, looked very pink in contrast to her yellowish skin, and she looked much older than her thirty-one years.

"I thought it was all up with me, Sister. I thought so until you talked to me about what they would do and how I would feel. It was just as you said. I had the prick in the arm down here and I felt on cloud nine . . . like I was high, although I can only guess what that's like. I don't remember the theatre at all and when I came round, I was only a little bit sick." She looked at the young student nurse who stood at the side of the bed listening. "You learn from her, Nurse . . . she'll teach you more than all them books. She knows what a woman like me needs to know and believe me, it made all the difference."

Anna shook her head, smiling. "It's true," insisted Sandra. "You watch all the sisters you work for, Nurse. This one can touch a pillow and it's right, while others nearly have you on the floor and you still feel uncomfortable afterwards!"

Anna laughed, "I think you're still on cloud nine, Sandra," but she noticed, with a strange sensation of pleased humility, that the little nurse seemed to agree with the patient. She thought back again to her own training, as she had done several times during the past few days of responsibility, and realised just how much was passed on from one generation of nurses to the next . . . expertise that could never be read up in textbooks. She finished her round and left the ward quiet and the patients free of pain.

It was a busy day. Two women in for investigation and tests, who had been in bed at the opening ceremony, went home and two more surgical cases took their places. This was going to be a very busy unit, Anna thought, and was conscious of the exhilaration and satisfaction of work well done. With the new admissions, only the side ward was empty and Sister Johnston's ward was also full. With any luck, the waiting list for gynaecological surgery would grow less in a very short time with twenty extra beds and the new theatre.

Anna was tired when she went off duty and almost wished that the dinner party was to be held on another evening. She shook out a full skirt, finely pleated and full of rich colours, and when she had showered and brushed her hair she dressed with her usual care, adding a long-sleeved silk blouse which glowed blue-green in the lamplight and seemed to find the echo of colour reflected in her dark hair. The neckline of the blouse seemed to need a finishing touch, and she slipped a fine gold chain over her head, letting the locket nestle in the folds of the blouse over her bosom.

Susan tapped on her door. She was ready, and her eyes sparkled. "With luck, we should have an undisturbed night. Sister from the main theatre said she would take any emergencies tonight, and Night Sister has sent a very experienced staff nurse to the wards. What it is to be Sir Horace and to wave a magic wand! I'm really looking forward to some decent nosh and a good bottle of wine." She listened. "Any sound from across the way?"

"I haven't noticed," Anna said.

"Now, then, stop clamming up as soon as he is

mentioned. What gives with you two? Anyone would think there was a feud between you."

"I don't know. Ask him, if you're so curious. I think he's plain anti-social. I expect he'll do a round of the wards and go to bed with a good book," Anna said acidly.

"Well, I hope Sir Horace has a little talent lined up for us!" enthused Susan.

"And you on the verge of marriage? You are a fickle woman, Sister Johnston," said Anna with a smile.

"I can look, even if I mustn't touch!" They picked up their coats and evening bags and went quickly to the entrance where a taxi waited. "So silly, but Sir Horace insisted that it might rain and now, I'm glad he sent a car." Susan glanced down at her dainty strip sandals and out at the dark puddles forming under a leaden sky. "Will it ever be Spring? We have one glimpse and then it rains again."

But the air was fresh and clean-washed and the scent of green leaves came to them through the gloom, and when they entered the foyer of the restaurant, they gasped at the lovely display of flowers on the reception desk. A mass of jonquils and daffodils were backdropped by dark green house plants, and bowls of crocus and hyacinths completed the heady mass of Spring.

"How marvellous," said Anna and bent to smell the flowers, her eyes half-shut.

"I didn't think you cared for flowers." A cold voice made her straighten. Slade Forsythe was not looking as grim as usual. His eyes were sad and belied the chill of his words, but Anna heard only the voice before she turned away and said she wanted to leave her coat in the cloakroom. It was impossible for him to know if she had heard him, or even knew that he was there. Only Susan saw the tightening of Anna's face as she swept past him.

I hope he isn't going to ruin the evening for Anna, Susan thought, and wondered why two perfectly reasonable human beings could have such an adverse effect on each other.

She smiled, and Slade Forsythe seemed to come to life. He started, and fingered the heavy silk tie he wore with the well-cut suit. Susan thought how handsome he looked and stifled a slightly guilty feeling that she was comparing him with her fiancé, whom she loved dearly, but whom she knew was certainly no Adonis.

Slade walked into the room with her to meet Sir Horace and Lady Ritchie. He brought her a glass of sherry and made himself as charming as any man could do, and when Anna saw them from the doorway they were chatting easily and she had the sensation that she was excluded until Sir Horace came forward. He began exclaiming on the colour of her blouse and flirting shamelessly with her, to the amusement of his wife, who had watched this little interchange so often whenever a pretty young thing entered her husband's orbit.

Four other guests arrived, then Matron, elegant and rather imposing in dark brown silk and good gold earrings, with one of the senior physicians. Lady Ritchie glanced round the room and frowned. She made a remark to her husband and he looked at the guests. "You're right, my dear. One missing. We can't go in until the table is complete." He was looking cross, as if he were a child who had been offered an apple and then had it snatched away before he could eat it.

"We aren't late," his wife said, in a placating voice. "Have another sherry while we wait." But he waved aside the tray offered by the waiter. Lady Ritchie looked at Matron and turned down the corners of her mouth. It needed so little to take the edge off the enjoyment of what might have been a perfect evening.

"Ah . . . there he is," said Sir Horace and glanced at his watch as if to check if the latecomer was really late. His face cleared. "Right on time, young man . . . another minute and we'd have gone in without you . . . and closed the door."

For a moment the surgeon showed, the man who ruled his firm with a kindly rod of iron; but iron, for all that. Then, he was the genial host, eager to entertain and to make his guests welcome.

"Come, my dear," he said to Anna, "you look pale. Faint for lack of food, eh, what? We'll soon put that right. I'm looking after you tonight." He held out his arm and Anna was genuinely glad to take it.

He saw her fluttering eyelashes and thought she looked like a brightly coloured, trapped bird, trembling before her captor. He squeezed her arm and she looked up gratefully. What has the young bounder been doing, he thought, to make such a lovely girl react like that? And as they found their seats, with Anna at the right hand of Sir Horace and Susan at his left, he watched the handsome man who made up the last of the party. The man invited by Lady Ritchie who had chanced to meet him in the West End of London and asked him to visit them for old times' sake. . . . Dr. Rob Delaney, who had left two years ago.

Anna regained her composure, thankful that Rob was at the far end of the table. It was almost a relief to have Slade Forsythe sitting by her side, even though he was deep in conversation with Matron who sat at his other side. The food was good but Anna picked at it, her appetite gone.

Sir Horace filled her wine-glass and whispered, "I don't know what's wrong, my dear, but you must eat. Have some wine and relax," and soon, the warmth of the room, the good wine and the growing feeling that she could handle the situation, made her eat and talk naturally.

Slade Forsythe turned to her and made small talk. Did he sense that she had relaxed? Did he know why she had looked so shocked? It was impossible to guess, but Anna knew that he had seen her reaction when Rob Delaney entered the room. For a long moment she looked into the grey eyes and found in them kindliness, sympathy and something more that made her catch her breath.

She lowered her eyelids and Slade Forsythe saw the delicate sweep of dark lashes on the pale cheeks and the gentle curve of her mouth. In that moment, an unwilling rapport blossomed between them, and although a moment later they were talking of trivial subjects, it remained like a glowing, warming spark between them.

He must feel as I do, thought Anna. No wonder he seems cold and cynical whenever we meet. I must seem the same to him. We have a bitter memory which we share. I have my heartbreaking rejection by Rob, and Slade Forsythe has the knowledge that it was his girlfriend, Carmel, who went away with Rob. We share rejection, and it is a shared humiliation.

Stealing another glance at the strong, good-looking face, she knew that such rejection would have hit his pride even more than it would a lesser man's, a man without his looks, attractiveness and status. Each time he sees me, she thought, he recalls the days with Carmel, just as he reminds me of Rob. But tonight they were there together, Rob Delaney and Slade Forsythe. Only Carmel was missing.

"Seeing you here, together, reminds me of so much," said Lady Ritchie with her usual sweet concern, but also with her usual complete lack of tact. "How is that beautiful girl who left at the same time as you did, Rob? What was her name? Carmen?"

"Carmel," said a low voice at Anna's side. She glanced at his face, but Slade Forsythe was sipping Chablis and his eyes were hooded.

Sir Horace coughed loudly but his wife took no notice. She liked to think that she knew all the hospital gossip and could show that she cared about the staff, past and present. "I remember . . . Carmel. Such a very pretty girl. I thought you were going to marry her at one time, Slade."

She looked at his expressionless face and knew that she had said the wrong thing. "But of course, she had two strings to her bow, didn't she?" Her face became pink as she realised that with every word she was sinking deeper into a situation that was sure to cause embarrassment. "I mean . . ." she laughed in a rather forced manner. "Such a lovely girl is bound to have many admirers." She saw Anna's face and remembered that she had been involved. "Oh, dear," she said, "I'm very sorry . . . I just can't keep up with all your doings . . . take no notice of me."

A voice from the other end of the table came crisply through the uneasy silence. "Carmel is in South America with her family," said Rob. For the first time, he stared directly at Anna. "She has gone there to marry an immensely wealthy cattle owner." He said it

55

slowly and with no sadness. It was as if he was reading an item in the newspaper concerning an acquaintance of little interest but some curiosity value. "She left three months ago," he added.

Anna sat very still. A buzz of interested talk followed Rob's statement, but for her, the room was empty except for her and Rob and the strong, dark shadow at her side. The three of them were connected by an intangible thread that bound them up with the past . . . and perhaps the future.

Slade Forsythe murmured something and filled her glass with wine. He passed her the silver dish of petits fours, and when she took no notice of the dish he touched her hand and said in a harsh whisper, "Don't worry, we can do without them, can't we? Try to relax. You've done so well, don't spoil your record by showing your feelings in public."

His suffering came to her through the mist of memory and acute awareness of the man at the other end of the table. "Have a gooey sweet," he said in a more normal voice.

Anna smiled up at Slade, an almost tender interest in her eyes. "Thank you, you broke the spell. I felt like a trapped rabbit," she whispered.

"Do you mind that she has left him?" he said, under cover of a sudden burst of laughter.

"I don't know," said Anna. "Did you know about Carmel?"

"No, why should I?" He smiled. "I know! Everyone thought that there was something between us, but it pleased me to let them think so." Anna looked at him and felt her first feelings of dislike return. "It was convenient to go out with her but there was nothing in

56

the affair that mattered. In fact, it was never a love affair," he added. "Anyone falling for Carmel needs to watch out. She'd eat them whole."

"Just because she rejected you doesn't allow you to talk about her like that. Do you talk of all your lady loves, I should say *ex*-lady friends like that?"

He grinned. "It was a useful cover-up for my real feelings for another girl, but who in their right mind would wear his heart on his sleeve in this hotbed of gossip . . . especially when Lady Ritchie gets it all wrong?"

"I don't believe you," said Anna.

"You'd better. It's true." but he did not name a name or hint at the identity of the woman he loved. A strange, uncomfortable man, thought Anna, a mixture of many disturbing facets to his character. In the wards he was adored by all the patients and most of the staff; with Carmel he had been attentive, and surely he had been in love with her? But with Anna, this was the first time that he had shown any humanity and now he had spoiled it again by pretending that to him Carmel was just another easy conquest.

At least he might have the decency to take defeat with dignity, she thought, and turned away to ask Sir Horace about the new house he was planning for his family in Surrey.

As she turned, Anna dropped her bag and Slade picked it up. "Put it on the table," he said firmly. "You'll lose it."

She took it from him and he still held it for long enough for her to feel a tug. He was giving her the bag but demanding that she look at him. The grey eyes were gentle.

"If you need me, remember that I am your neigh-

57

bour," he said, and turned to Matron on his other side.

Anna was aware of Rob all the time that Sir Horace talked of tree-planting, and of the new super greenhouse with automatic air conditioning that he planned. "I'm thinking of my retirement," he said. Anna looked shocked. "Nice of you to look surprised, my dear," he chuckled, "but Anno Domini catches us all in the end." He lowered his voice. "To tell you the truth, I'm looking foward to it. Celia loves the country and is much happier messing about with church and W.I. affairs than she is living in London. I shall dress in baggy cords and have a very large unmanageable dog!" he said with satisfaction.

Anna laughed. "I can't imagine you looking like that . . . or having anyone or anything that wouldn't obey you instantly. See how frightened your poor house surgeon is of you. He drops his notes and stammers every time you look in his direction."

Sir Horace laughed. "He's beginning to get to know my ways. He isn't a Beattie's man, or he'd know when I mean business and when I'm bluffing. It's a great game, my dear, but sometimes, I admit, a bit mean. However, it does assure me of efficiency, and none of us can afford to be other than efficient in our job, can we?" His manner was warm and fatherly.

"I'm glad to see a little colour in your cheeks," he continued. "I'm afraid that my wife did not realise that you might be embarrassed to meet that young man again. Tell me," he whispered, "who is your new boyfriend?"

"I haven't one! Once bitten, twice shy, as they say. I find I can do without men. I like my work, and the new unit is great." She smiled up at him and he almost believed her, but he noticed that she avoided looking at

Rob and didn't seem very keen to turn away to the handsome young man on her other side.

Music played softly and a curtain was drawn back, revealing the dance floor used by the main restaurant and the private room. The table was pushed aside and reduced to smaller units where the guests could sit in comfortable chairs and watch the modest cabaret. Slade Forsythe happened to be at the same small table where Anna had been placed by Sir Horace.

He ordered more coffee and asked her if she wanted a liqueur, but she said that she had drunk enough wine and would prefer to drink coffee. She could understand Sir Horace being protective, she thought, but surely that was alien to Slade Forsythe's nature? He was cool and aloof again, but she was acutely aware of him as a strong force against which it would be unwise for any outside influence to try and push too hard.

A ripple of applause made Anna start guiltily, as she had not looked at the floor show. The music began again, and she saw Rob stand up and look towards her. Couples were dancing and her heart beat faster with a mixture of dread and bitter-sweet anticipation. "Come," said a firm voice and Slade Forsythe put a hand under her elbow to guide her on to the dance floor.

To her horror, the music was an old, smoochy tune, a slow dance and not the impersonal detached shrugging of modern dances. Slade Forsythe put a hand round her waist and held her firmly, dancing well and guiding her effortlessly as if they had danced together many times. Anna smiled and began to enjoy herself.

Funny how the old dances are good once they get going, she thought. Strange that I feel so right with this cold man. I would never have given him credit for such a smooth performance. The music quickened, and again their steps fitted. Slade grinned. "I think the thing to say is 'do you come here often?' "

"Not often," she smiled, and once more that elusive glow started between them. Slade Forsythe stiffened and Anna nearly stumbled.

"May I cut in?" said a familiar voice.

"Must you? For God's sake get lost," said Slade, his voice low but full of anger.

"Yes, I must," said Rob Delaney, and smiled at Anna. "Hello," he said, "it's been a long time."

Anna gave Slade a scared glance then regained her composure. To her relief, the music was now belting out a rock number and she stood well away from her partner, spinning to avoid his touch. The music ended and she nodded slightly and almost raced back to safety between Slade and Sir Horace . . . but Sir Horace was at the bar, talking to the other consultant, and Slade was cornered by Lady Ritchie.

"What's the hurry?" said Rob, sinking into Sir Horace's chair and offering her a cigarette, raising his eyebrows when she refused coldly. "Not still angry with me? I've been away a long time, Anna."

She remained silent, unable to trust her voice. His eyes still held the look that had made her love him; his hair still fell carelessly over one eye when he forgot to push it away from his face, and his voice still did perilous things to her heart. But she appeared cool and her hands lay on the bright skirt as if she were completely relaxed. He seemed at a loss for a moment, then leaned forward and deliberately kissed her hand, holding it tightly so that she could not tear it away. She trembled and looked down, and he smiled his triumph.

The room was dimly lit and the others were dancing or talking. She was trapped in the corner and trapped in the agony of her own mixed-up feelings. Why had he come back to torment her? Why come into her life just as she was picking up the threads of living again?

"I had to come," he said, simply. "I found out where you were and I couldn't keep away."

"No, Rob!"

"Yes, Anna." The music stopped and the lights brightened as waiters came with more coffee and more drinks, and Sir Horace demanded his seat.

"Sorry, sir . . . but I had to renew an old friendship." Rob stood and laughed softly. "Please sit down, Sir Horace, I can come back later to carry on where I left off." His bold blue eyes were alive with triumph and anticipation but he was in no hurry to follow up his advantage. He walked away to the bar.

"What a lovely bright colour you have, dear," said Lady Ritchie.

Her husband growled something unintelligible and looked at his watch. His heavy brows came together in a frown. "It's time we went home," he said. Anna looked apprehensive. "Mr. Forsythe," he called and from the shadows, he came as if expecting the summons. "You will please see Sister Boswell safely back to her quarters. Sister Johnston will stay, and Matron can include her in her party when she goes."

Anna smiled weakly. How could she refuse when the great man spoke in that way? Slade was smiling, too, and bowed with mock humility. "She's tired, man . . . she needs looking after," said Sir Horace.

"I quite agree," returned Slade, and Anna's heart beat quietly once more. For all his faults, his arrogance and cynicism, he would never hurt her; of that she was certain. What a pity she didn't like him more than she did.

They slipped away as the lights dimmed for another old tune. Sir Horace had asked the group to play some of his favourites. As Slade put her coat round her shoulders the throaty words came to them, sung by a girl in a shimmering dress with long, smoky grey hair. '. . . you will see a stranger across a crowded room . . . once you have found her, never let her go, once you have found her, never let her go.'

The firm hands tightened for a second on her shoulders, and as Anna gazed across the room she could have almost convinced herself that a man's lips brushed her hair. "Come along," said Slade, "Cinderella's coach is waiting."

"I don't want to drag you away," protested Anna, "I can walk back . . . or take a taxi."

"You heard what the man said. Have you ever tried to do anything that Sir Horace says he does not favour?" His face was inscrutable, but his eyes twinkled.

"I can't imagine you doing anything that you didn't want to do," said Anna.

"You'd be surprised," he said lightly. The air was cold after the hot restaurant and Anna pulled her coat tightly round her. "Shall I bring the car nearer?"

She shook her head. "I wondered . . ." he began, and she was amazed at the uncertainty of his voice. "Would you like a quick drive . . . if you are warm enough? Blow away a few lungfuls of smoke?" He piloted her away from puddles and opened the car door. She sank into the low leather seat and sighed her thankfulness.

"Shall we go?" She nodded. "That would give me a lot of pleasure," he said formally, and she wondered how much he was doing for duty and how much he was in earnest, but now it didn't matter. She had a breathing space away from those bold, blue eyes and that dynamic personality.

He drove without talking and she didn't notice where they were going. It was good to sit there beside a man who had firm control of his powerful sports car, was in control of his life, his emotions and his future. She sighed. If only she could be as confident.

He heard her sigh. "Tired?"

"No, I'm enjoying the drive. I'm unwinding. It was good of you to bring me." She laughed. "But as you say, Sir Horace manages people."

He drove the car between tall dark gateposts. "This was my idea," he said. "I thought you'd had enough."

Anna sat up and stared. "We're in St. James's Park!" She smiled. "I've never been here as late as this. Surely even the ducks must be asleep?"

"Not the place for a girl on her own, but I think it has a kind of magic late at night."

He parked and they walked along the fast-drying paths by the lake. Across the night, bright trails of red flashed between the trees as the slow line of late cars left the glow of rear lights reflected in the wet black roads. Half-open leaves swayed and dripped gently, and the windows of the palace glowed in the distance.

"It's beautiful," said Anna. Slade said little and she was grateful. It was so good to absorb the atmosphere without bothering with words. If Rob were here, she thought, he would be saying amusing things, telling her stories that he could tell her anywhere, in a crowded pub, in the car, in the sitting-room of the medical school, or anywhere he could have her undivided attention. He would never just . . . be. He would talk or kiss her, not just the friendly kisses that said 'I love you and one day perhaps we'll marry'. His kisses had always been searching, passionate, wanting more than she was prepared to give at that stage in their love.

He rushed me, she thought with a remembered resentment. He wanted everything now, and could not savour the beauty of small things, brief moments. She imagined him in Dublin. He would have enjoyed the social life, the bars and the good Irish talk, but she doubted if he had explored the countryside, unless of course Carmel had made him do so.

The haze of blue-grey that is London and no other city, found shadows in the still water. A delinquent duck, out long after bedtime, gave a restless call as if a fox was near. "Do they have foxes in London?" said Anna.

They leaned on the bridge. "Foxes? They have them in many cities now. I don't know about London, but a friend of mine is trying to assess how many there are holed up in suburban gardens in Bristol." Slade dropped a piece of bread into the water. "Never can resist pinching bread from a dinner party. I usually come for a drive and find a pond or something."

"The ducks are asleep," laughed Anna, "but they'll have a nice surprise in the morning. Breakfast in bed."

"I love this park," he said, and they walked again. Anna found that they were going back towards the car and she suddenly wanted the night to go on. Her shattered calm was becoming whole again, except for a couple of jigsaw pieces that still fitted badly. Another hour and I can face Beattie's again, she thought. She saw him glancing at her shoes.

"My sister would be furious with me," he said.

"Your sister? Hospital or real?"

"My sister at home. She says that I never deserve to take a girl walking. If they wear pretty sandals, I usually manage to make them walk through ploughed fields or mud. She asks now, when I say I'll call for her, if it's a wellie-walk, or are we going somewhere civilised . . . and then she brings the other pair just in case."

He was smiling naturally and Anna sensed the warmth of his family. If only he were like this all the time . . . but he must have brought Carmel here. Was that why he had good vibrations, tender memories in this park? To her horror, she found that it mattered. She hated to think of Carmel with him, here.

"I'm hungry," he said.

"You can't be!"

"But you are . . . you ate very little this evening." He unlocked the car. "If I didn't remember what my sister told me, you'd have walked, young woman! But in deference to her, I'll drive you to the embankment and we can drink a cup of coffee with the cream of London society."

They went to an all-night coffee stand overlooking the river. The monosyllabic man serving pushed huge mugs of coffee towards them, and thick wodgy sandwiches.

"I know now where you find your bread for the birds," said Anna. "I can't eat all of this." But she did, and even accepted a bar of chocolate to eat as they watched the grey shapes of boats, softly lit and gliding like ghosts along the artery of London.

Big Ben struck the hour. "What would Sir Horace say?" said Slade. It was three o'clock and the road south across the bridge and down to Camberwell Green was nearly deserted. From the river, hooters made an

65

early morning call and Anna knew that in some strange way the dark man who drove so well, his face almost harsh in repose, had helped her more than anyone could have done, by saying nothing.

The hospital was quiet, the doors of Casualty closed. "I can't smell an emergency, can you?" said Anna. He smiled. "I want to thank you," she began, the words stumbling, "I want to say . . ."

He led her to the entrance to the nurses' home and put his key in the lock. "You are to say nothing. There is nothing for which you have to thank me. It was a pleasure."

But from his cool tone, she wondered if the whole outing had been a plot, an order from Sir Horace to keep her out late so that Rob could not see her again that night. Softly they walked up the main staircase to avoid disturbing the sleeping staff. At her door, Anna opened her evening bag and took out her room key.

"I still want to thank you," she persisted. "I enjoyed the last part of the evening very much . . . more than I can say," she whispered.

Slade took her key and unlocked her door. He handed her the key and she looked up, startled at the exquisite sensation that was part pain and was wholly awareness, as his fingers touched her hand.

"Be careful," he said. His face was expressionless and once more, almost harsh as he took her face in his hands and kissed her on the mouth, so gently that it left her breathless, wondering if it had happened.

He pushed her gently into her room and closed the door, and in another moment she heard the door opposite her own close quietly, and Anna found the tears of release salty on her lips.

CHAPTER FOUR

ANNA woke late, her first thought being of relief that it was a day off duty, and then she remembered the evening and the dinner party when Sir Horace and his wife had entertained them at the Falcon. The early morning bustle of the nurses' home had died into the spasmodic rattle of buckets and vacuum cleaners as the day's work began. The woman who cleaned the room had come in and Anna had murmured, "Day off".

It was her own fault, she thought. She hadn't left the *Do not Disturb* notice on her door. Then she remembered why it had slipped her mind.

A faint tingling spread through her body as she recalled the soft touch of Slade Forsythe's lips on hers. It had been a kiss so gentle, so undemanding that now it seemed impossible that a man of his force of character could have been so restrained . . . but of course, to him it was like a handshake, an expected gesture, just enough to show a girl that she was attractive and he'd enjoyed her company, but not enough to give her any illusions of a grand passion lurking under his cool façade.

She turned on the shower. If he was in love . . . really in love with a woman, it must be quite, quite something, she thought, then cooled the heady thought with a dousing of ice-cold water. "Serve you right for prying into his fantasies," she said, and was amazed how cheerful and rested she was.

She would go to Harrod's, have some lunch and see the new exhibition at the National Gallery, and meet

Monica Johns, the sister from men's surgical for the evening. She tried not to think of Rob and his thinly veiled threat that he intended pursuing her again, and this time making her do as he wished. Last night it had taken her by surprise, but she was confident that he must be going on his way very soon, and if she could keep out of his way he might get the message that she had stopped loving him and never wanted to see him again.

The windows looked very dirty. Anna realised that this was because the sun was shining brilliantly outside, and it showed the accumulation of grime that never quite left the windows however many times they were cleaned. In the corridor dust hung in a sunbeam, and she thought of her grandmother's old house where they called such beams fairy gold.

She glanced at the closed door of Slade's room and remembered that he was going to Guy's to see a surgical procedure which interested him; so today, if Sir Horace had a hangover, it would be Susan Johnston's lot to bear with him and his bad temper. As for the poor little house surgeon . . . her lips twitched with amusement.

Claud was at his post, with the inevitable mug of brown-skinned tea in his cubby-hole. "Something funny Sister?" he asked hopefully, thinking that Sister Anna, as he called her behind her back, looked very dishy . . . very dishy indeed. "I got some more stamps if you want any," he said. "Going up West? Don't get picked up by one of them rich Arabs, Sister. Can't have nice girls like you being put in one of them arums."

"I don't think I'm the type for an Eastern harem, Claud," she said firmly.

"Got enough troubles near at hand, like?" He winked.

"Certainly not," she retorted. "I am another Florence Nightingale, and when I'm Matron of Beattie's, you'd better treat me with more respect!"

"Garn!" he said, comfortably. "You'll never make it."

"So you think I'm not good enough?" she laughed.

"Oh, not that, Sister." He looked shocked. "You're good, everyone says so, but with all those good-looking medicos around, you'll be spliced before you know where you are."

"I haven't noticed many!"

"Get away . . . what about last night, then?"

"I went out to dinner with a party at the invitation of Sir Horace and his wife. He isn't the one you think is dying of love for me, surely?"

"Friend of mine . . ."

Anna groaned. "All right . . . a friend of yours was in the Falcon and saw that at least four of the men were not in wheelchairs and could be called attractive. Two were already engaged."

Claud looked sly, wondering just how far he could go. "What about the others?" Anna blushed. "Dr. Delaney was there, wasn't he?"

"He was in the same party," she said, coldly. "And while we're talking about Dr. Delaney, I'd be glad if you would not tell him anything about my off duty or what I'm doing."

Claud looked uncomfortable. "Beat you to it, Sister. He came in early." He gestured towards the entrance. "He's out there with his car."

"Damn, damn, damn!" Anna's eyes flashed fire. She

grabbed her stamps and ran back towards the nurses' home, tripped on the top step and was grabbed as she fell. Slade Forsythe held her close for an instant and led her inside. "Thank you," she said shakily.

"My pleasure . . . just your friendly neighbourhood jack-of-all-trades." He grinned. "I didn't know the wine at the Falcon was so long-lasting in its potency. Or was it the coffee on the embankment? Now, that was a bit sinister."

He's giving me time to recover again, she thought. "Well, thank you," she repeated.

"I was going out," said Slade Forsythe, "can I give you a lift?" Her relief must have shown. "I can? Good! Got a train to catch . . . or were the goblins chasing you?" He was polite and mildly humorous, as he would be with any woman he knew slightly.

"I was going to Harrod's, but anywhere along the way will do. I can take a bus or the underground once I'm clear of Camberwell."

"This way," he said, and went to his car. He turned, and to Anna's surprise he went to the far entrance and turned out of the main gates which led on to the road, instead of taking the short cut by Claud's lodge and through the gateway where Rob Delaney was waiting. As they passed the road junction, Slade glanced in his mirror and chuckled. Rob stood nonchalantly by his car, smoking a cigarette.

"He'll have a long wait, unless Claud tells him," he said.

"You knew he was there?"

"I came out earlier and saw him." His hands tightened on the steering wheel. "We talked."

Anna felt a rush of sympathy for the man at her side.

He must have felt terrible about being reminded of Carmel, whatever he said to hide his true feelings for the beautiful vibrant girl who had run off with Rob to Ireland.

"I thought you needed a little more time to get used to the idea that he's back in town. You must be very sure before you become involved with him again, Anna."

Once more, she was conscious of his strength. It's the first time he's called me Anna, she thought. Even spoken in that matter-of-fact, almost brotherly way, it was good to hear and seemed more important than anything else he was saying.

"I'll be careful . . . but he's just passing through. I'm sure he has plans that don't include me," she said with more conviction than she felt.

They sped over Westminster Bridge and turned off. Slade glanced at his watch, and Anna remembered that he had an appointment. "I mustn't make you late for Guy's," she said. "What are you doing there?"

He explained that the surgeon wanted to try out a tissue graft to stop inflamed surfaces from clinging together and forming adhesions in the abdomen. She frowned. "Many surgeons have their own ways of doing that. What's so new about your method?"

By the time he dropped her off near Harrod's, they were engrossed in technical details and it was with regret that Anna said her thanks and goodbyes, but parking being what it was in London, he could do no more than smile and finish in mid-sentence before filtering into the traffic again.

Anna watched him go and half wished that she could go with him. Ridiculous! Days off were for relaxing, enjoying the big outside world and forgetting the inevitable tensions created by responsibility and illness.

The day passed pleasantly. With a strange sensation of nostalgia for the previous night, Anna fed the ducks in St. James's and watched the tiny sparrows alighting five or six at a time on the hands of enchanted tourists. The blue-green and crimson of the ducks' plumage against the grey-green water under the weeping willows made a picture that filled her with pleasure. So, this was the big, impersonal city . . . it was beautiful. She laughed at two ducks who dived for the same morsel.

I must tell Slade, she thought, and remembered with a pang that she might not have the opportunity to do so. He has done his duty, she thought. The next time I see him will be on the ward or in the operating theatre. When he asks for forceps, I can hardly say, "By the way, there were these two ducks . . ." And she was sad as she crumbled the last of the biscuits for the noisy birds.

The exhibition was disappointing, or was it that she found the high-windowed gallery oppressive? It was better to see the real birds, the real trees, than anything on canvas; but she stood by a bronze figure of Mercury, messenger of the gods, and admired the fine, clean lines of the athletic body. He would look like that . . . but she wouldn't admit to herself that she was thinking of Slade.

Monica Johns was late. Anna walked back to the entrance of the underground, acutely aware of the appraising glances of passing men. She waited a while, looking at the magazines on a stall and then bought an evening paper. She hated waiting and was becoming cross. If Monica was coming, why couldn't she be on time? She would be the first one to object to waiting.

Anna went out into the street again and looked to the right and then to the left. A man who was waiting too came towards her. Oh, no! That's all I need, she thought, turning away from him. If he tries to pick me up, I shall just go . . . and Monica can go to her precious film alone!

A shadow halted before her, and Anna looked up at the man's smiling face. "Rob!" she exclaimed. "What on earth are you doing here?"

"Let's go," he said.

She pulled away from his hand on her arm. "No, I'm waiting for someone."

"If it's Monica, you can forget it. I sent her off with Douglas, with tickets I had from a grateful patient who I happened to meet, and I said I'd try to console you for the loss of your evening's entertainment."

"No, Rob . . . please go. I don't want to come with you."

"Anna, I have no intention of brawling with you in public. If we don't smile and go quietly, that nice policewoman over there will think I've picked you up! You don't want to be had for soliciting, do you, darling?"

Her cheeks flamed, but she followed reluctantly. Only Rob would cheapen a woman by saying such a thing. Did she look like a tart?

She glanced at the profile of the man who could still have a disastrous effect on her resistance. Was it her imagination, or had it coarsened slightly during the two years they had been apart? His lips, full and sensual, and the hitherto endearing weakness of his chin, seemed more evident today. She matched her step to his and caught a glimpse of her reflection among the filmy lace of a bridal trousseau in a shop window. It showed a slim, well-dressed and very attractive girl. Her confidence rose.

"They are very sexy . . . didn't know you liked that sort of thing," said Rob, taking it that she was looking at the clothes.

"I don't," she said shortly.

"We can do without," he said with a lazy smile.

"Where are we going?" she demanded. "Because if you can't keep off that subject, I'll catch the first bus that comes along."

"I'm sorry." His smile mocked her, but held genuine admiration. "But you're prettier than ever, Anna. Let's eat and talk . . . we have a lot of talking to do."

They threaded their way through the evening crowds and Anna had time to notice how cosmopolitan London had become. When she was training at the Princess Beatrice Hospital she had been aware of many foreigners in the West End but never had she seen such fascinating clothes. They passed a group of Asians, the women aglow in beautiful silk saris, with huge limpid eyes and graceful postures. A Nigerian of Herculean build dominated a space among the pigeons in Trafalgar Square, and with his colourful robes looked as if he was there to tame Nelson's lions.

In spite of her anger at Rob's peremptory assumption that she would follow him, she could not avoid the lift of her heart that London gave her whenever the weather was fine and the crowds moved with a sense of urgency.

"No, not there!" Anna hung back from the entrance of a small restaurant on the side of a narrow street in Soho. It was the place where Rob had told her that he loved her. While they had eaten . . . what was it? At the time, she could not remember, but it was surely ambrosia and was it nectar they had drunk? It had been an enchanted evening, and she had believed that Rob was the love of her life for ever . . . she had taken all that he said in trust and love, and had never doubted that his declaration of love was the prelude to marriage as soon as it could be arranged.

Looking back, she recalled his silence when she had said, "I would like to finish my training before we are married, Rob. After all, it will be a useful qualification wherever we live and we can work together."

He had assured her that there was no rush . . . to put marriage out of her plans for the time, and to concentrate on being in love.

Anna had thought him to be kind and patient until she had finally got the message that he expected to become her lover in every sense of the word. The fact that she would not sleep with him had given rise to several rows, and when at last he had taunted her with heartlessness and frigidity and told her that he couldn't exist without sex, she had known that she wasn't the first love of his life, nor was she likely to be the last, even if she married him. Carmel had come at the moment when he was restive, looking round for an easy conquest and he, the man who was in control of his emotions, or so he believed, had fallen for Carmel and for once had met his match.

"No, Rob, that's all in the past," she said now. "I don't want to eat there."

"But you remember it," Rob said softly. "You remember and I remember, and neither of us will ever forget it if we live to be two hundred and fifty. Come on, it's time you faced up to me, Anna, because I've come back for you."

A shudder went through her whole body, but she allowed herself to be steered into the dimly lit restaurant. He took her coat from her shoulders and his hand brushed the curve of her breast. It was like an electric shock. The impact of his closeness, the awareness of his masculinity made her catch her breath, and she was glad to slide behind the seat of the leather banquette and hide her face in the shadow.

"It's changed," she said. She had a few precious moments in which to recover her poise while Rob found somewhere to put the coats. She gained courage. "It's changed," she repeated firmly. "Two years is too long, Rob. This place is under different management." She gave a mischievous smile. "You know what's on the menu? Unless you've changed a lot, you'll hate it!"

The waiter came and before Rob could say they'd made a mistake and come to the wrong place, Anna took the menu and ordered Chow Mein followed by lychees.

"Oh, yes, China tea, please . . . no wine for me," she said sweetly. "I want to keep a very clear head," she added softly, so that only Rob could hear.

Rob searched the menu for something resembling European food and hopefully ordered King Prawns without the sauce. "Not that they'll take the slightest notice," he said, "it will come smothered in some Chinese muck."

"You wanted to come here!" said Anna. "Thank

you, Rob, I adore Chinese food!" He sat in moody silence until the food came. Where was his master plan, of attack followed by food, wine and seduction, going? He could see the evening disintegrating as Anna tucked in to her spring rolls and Chow Mein. She wasn't even drinking wine, which would at least have had the effect of mellowing her, making her sentimental as he whispered of their mutual memories, words of love and promises for the future.

"We can go for coffee to a place I know," said Anna. "Really good coffee . . . or there was last week when I came up to look round the shops." She smiled. "Unless *that* has changed hands. Everything changes so quickly in the big city, doesn't it?"

They walked along Piccadilly and found the coffee house. Rob ordered Gaelic coffee for two without consulting her, and called the waiter back to order sandwiches. "I'm still starving," he said. "You know I hate Chinese food."

He said it as if it was her fault that he had gone there in the first place, and Anna began to remember many incidents when his petty bouts of bad temper had spoiled outings. It was a reprieve. Physically he was very attractive, and if she was alone with him where he could embrace her and tell her that he loved her, Anna knew that her will-power would be put to a very severe test. Could she resist this man, even though he had so nearly broken her heart? She sipped her coffee through the cool cream while Rob ate chicken sandwiches and regained his good temper.

"Now, this is good. I like it here," he said, as if the Chinese restaurant was a lapse of Anna's which he forgave, and now he was showing her where he *really* liked to spend an evening. She willed him to make more and more unfair judgements, to be even more disgruntled.

It is quite easy to dislike you . . . even if I still love you, she thought. She did not love Slade Forsythe, but there had been moments when she knew that under their surface animosity there lay a fellow-feeling on many subjects. However much he annoys me, I like him, she realised to her surprise. I am in love with Rob . . . or I think I am, but I like Slade Forsythe. He called me Anna, just once. "Sorry . . . I was far away," she said.

"I was asking if you'd like more coffee, or shall we go to that nice pub in St. James's? I could do with a real drink."

"Aren't you taking a risk? That might have changed too." .

"No," he said acidly, "I checked. I went there yesterday. That place will be there on Judgement Day."

"I'd rather stay here," Anna answered firmly. "I'll have plain coffee without Irish whiskey. You said we had some talking to do, and this place is quiet. Talk, Rob, and let's clear the air."

He gazed at her in amazement. Where was the quiet and rather docile girl he had known? Not that she had been docile over one thing, and he had been forced to admit that somewhere, she had a hint of steel that guarded her moral values.

But this was a woman, not a girl. This Anna had poise because she was a success in her work and carried her responsibility proudly. She was more difficult but much more desirable. He began to talk of the hospital and how he knew that he had missed an opportunity to become Senior House Officer to the medical team with which he had worked. "I regret that," he said, and shrugged.

"You took the job in Ireland and Carmel went with you." Her voice was controlled, but Anna's heart beat fast. She had to know, and it must all be said, so now was the time to say it all, to begin again or to finish their relationship for ever.

Rob turned his coffee-glass and stared into the creamy dregs. "I went to Ireland and the job was fine. It wasn't Beattie's, but it was good enough. Carmel managed to get a job in her own profession and we had a small flat on the outskirts of Dublin." He looked up and the blue eyes were hard. "Do you really need to know? It's over."

"You asked me to come. I do need to know if we are to be friends," she said.

"Friends? Come off it, Anna. We can never be friends. I know that, seeing you again, knowing that I've loved you all the time I was away."

It was easier to be calm and firm when he relapsed into the old technique, the same old easy words. "Any relationship that does not include friendship is not love," said Anna. "You set up house with Carmel and you lived together as lovers. I believed you had married her, but I suppose you told her, too, that there was plenty of time for that and that you should concentrate on loving?"

Her voice was edgy and her eyes shone, but not with happiness nor yet unshed tears. "What happened, Rob? Did she get tired of waiting, or did you find other women who interested you more?"

"No . . . she left me. She refused to marry me." He

couldn't meet her eyes. "I tell you, Anna, I longed for you so often when she went . . . I knew then that I had gone mad over her, but it wasn't love. You were right. I didn't really like her as an individual." He shrugged. "But she is very beautiful."

"Yes," said Anna, "beautiful enough to go through life taking men and then refusing to marry them when something better turns up. I suppose she jilted Slade Forsythe?"

He gave her a sharp look to see if she was joking. "Good God, no, not Forsythe! He never came into it except that he tried to occupy her time to keep me away from her. He knew her parents at one time, or his family did. He took his responsibilities seriously, and knowing that Latin families are strict with their women, he took her under his wing."

He laughed. "It was like taking a fully grown eagle under the wing of a dove! Carmel is all woman, and when she fancies a man it would take more than Slade Forsythe to protect her from her own desires." He looked at Anna with speculation. "I never believed that story. I think he had another reason for keeping me, in particular, away from Carmel."

Anna heard Slade's voice in her mind. He had said he had used Carmel as a cover for his feelings for another woman and she had not believed him, but if Rob was telling the truth, it made sense.

A cold corner formed in Anna's heart. Who was the other woman that Slade loved, so well-hidden that no one at Beattie's suspected anything? Was it a love that had never blossomed, never been declared? She tried to think who had been in the medical school two years ago, and who of the right age had been on the nursing staff, but she could think of no one with whom Slade's name had been linked. It would account for the bitter line of the young surgeon's mouth when he was tired, and in her heart, she knew that he was worth two of Rob Delaney.

"And now? Where is Carmel?"

"There was an unholy row and she walked out on me. One night, she took everything while I was on duty and left a note saying the equivalent of 'it was fun while it lasted'. I must have been blind! She was doing physio in the private patients' block and met this wealthy South American. Although she is of mixed Latin and English blood, physically and mentally, Carmel is not English. He asked her to marry him and go back to South America, and as soon as he was well they were married by a priest in Ireland." He shrugged. "Our Puritan friend Slade Forsythe must be relieved. At least she has gone back to her family and a very well heeled future, all in one piece . . . if a trifle shop-soiled. South American families of substance like their new brides to be virgins." He spoke with contempt.

"And men like you try their best to take that away. Really, Rob, you are very old-fashioned!" He stared.

"You might think you belong to a new society where love should be free," Anna told him contemptuously, "but you know that once a woman has lost her virtue even men like you despise them. Yet you try to retain the Victorian idea of one rule for men and one for women." She smiled sadly. "There comes a time for us all when we have to decide what we really want, and not to chase butterflies."

He took her hand. "I want you, Anna. I know now that I was a fool to go away." His voice grew husky and

81

his mouth slightly moist. "God, you're lovely . . . if you only knew how much I want you at this minute."

She drew away. "You want me, Rob, as you want other luxuries, to enjoy and to forget. I'm not built like that. If I go to someone, it will be for good."

"Then come to me, Anna. Come to me tonight, and I swear we'll be married whenever you say. I love you, and I'm asking you to marry me."

"But you want me tonight?" Her voice was brittle.

"I can't wait until we're married. I need you now. Oh, Anna, it's so good to be with you again." He put an arm round her, and she stiffened.

"Not going all frigid on me again, are you?" he demanded. "Anna . . . surely there must have been someone when I went away? You haven't lived like a nun all this time? I don't believe it. Not with your face and figure."

Anna smiled. "I'd like that drink," she said, "you can get one here if you go into the adjoining bar."

He gave an exclamation of delight, rose and went through to the other bar. Anna quickly fetched her coat and left, running to the tube station and sinking breathlessly on to a seat as the doors closed. She passed a weary hand over her face. He was bad . . . but so beautiful, and flight was her only salvation.

She was mentally exhausted when she stepped out of the tube station. The hospital was a long way off, and the thought of walking in the dark through a run-down district was unattractive to one who had used all her reserve of strength and fortitude, so she waited at the taxi rank for ten minutes until the queue had cleared and a cab was available. She shared the taxi with a young couple going as far as Camberwell, the girl heavily pregnant and quite incapable of walking far.

Anna wondered if she would meet her again and fervently hoped that she wouldn't, for the girl was looking forward to a normal delivery and Anna knew that if she came into her ward it would mean that something was wrong. The taxi continued up the hill, into quieter streets and the lights of the hospital came into view.

To Anna's surprise, the driver refused a tip. "Got a lot to thank Beattie's for, Nurse," he said. "Any time you want a car, ring me." He handed her a card. "My wife was took real bad last year and had to have it all out."

Anna made a mental translation. The local patients referred to any operation which involved the womb or ovaries in that way.

"In the old building with Sister Styles it was," the man continued. "Never thought I'd see her looking as she does now, Nurse. Plays with the grandchildren, cooks for the family and does all her own housework. It was a real miracle."

He waved as he left, and once more Anna had a feeling of humility. People remembered, and it took her by surprise. She *was* doing a good job, in spite of the sneering way that Rob treated all mention of dedication and a career that mattered. She glanced at her watch. It had taken a long time to get back to Beattie's and it was very late. The front door to the nurses' home was open and she did not need to use her key. She checked the pigeon-hole that bore her name in case she had missed a message or a letter from home, and she found a postcard from a friend on holiday.

She read it as she climbed the stairs, smiling as she

83

pictured Melanie, a girl from her home town, trying to find enough sun in Spain to get a tan when it was, as she said, raining stair-rods. Anna reached the corridor leading to her room and looked up, sensing that she was not alone.

"And where the hell do you think you've been?" said Rob.

"How did you get in here?" Anna could hardly believe it. This was the nurses' home where men did not enter. But of course, it was different now. If people like Slade Forsythe were allowed rooms here, what was there to prevent any of the medical staff from coming into the place?

"I was frantic," said Rob, "I looked all over that bloody coffee house and even got some funny looks as I lurked outside the powder room. Then the waitress said you'd left in a tearing hurry and I knew that little Anna, the good girl of Beattie's, had stood me up!" His voice was cold and menacing. "So you couldn't stand the heat? Even little Anna felt a flicker of feeling for a man, and she was scared out of her tiny mind." He sat on the oak settle at the end of the corridor, with the caution of one who is unsure of his balance.

"You're drunk," said Anna in disgust.

"Drunk? Well, what do you expect? I go for a drink and come back thinking I had it made for tonight, and find you've chickened out."

"I didn't say you could come here. I didn't say anything except that I'd like you to go to fetch me a drink." She noticed that his eyes were rimmed with red as if he had drunk a lot, and she also remembered that Rob grew quarrelsome when he had too much whiskey.

"Rob," she said gently. "I'm sorry. I panicked and

84

ran. I thought everything was moving too fast and I was afraid.''. He smiled unpleasantly. "Go to bed, Rob, and we'll talk tomorrow." He did not move. "Will you go if I make you some black coffee.''

"In there?" He pointed to the nearest bedroom, which happened to be Slade's.

"That's not my room." She thought quickly. "I don't live on this floor," she lied, knowing that once she let Rob into her room there would be no security for her. "I'll make coffee in the kitchen and we can drink it in the sitting-room. The chairs are comfortable there."

"Where's your room?"

"You'd never make it, Rob. It's up two more flights and the lift doesn't work at night." He swayed to his feet. "Come on, black coffee," said Anna, firmly, as if trying to persuade a patient to take medicine that was essential but unpleasant. "I make very good coffee," she said, and smiled.

"That damned Chinese food," complained Rob. *And* half a bottle of whiskey, thought Anna. He lurched after her to the stairs and followed her down, holding on to the banister rail as if he were on a boat tossing in a force six gale. By the time he had made it to the deepest armchair, Anna had the kettle nearly boiling and was looking for coffee-mugs. She put instant coffee into two mugs and handed him a mug, half-filled. He promptly spilled some, but greedily drank the rest and demanded more. She gave him even stronger coffee and he seemed to recover his equilibrium.

They sat for a while, with Rob casting reproachful glances at her but saying little, but she gathered that he had to make up his mind about a job he'd been offered in Canada. "You must come with me, Anna. Say you'll

85

come. I have to tell them in a day or so and leave soon after, if I'm going."

"Do you think you'll be happy in Canada, Rob?"

"If you'll come, I'll be happy anywhere," he said. "I do love you, Anna. I only got drunk tonight because I was so mad. I want to marry you, on any terms you like, I was a fool to think you were like Carmel."

He was sobering fast, and Anna felt an upsurge of compassion for this weak but lovable man. "I promise you I will be good," he said, "I'll go to bed now." He wagged a finger at her. "Do as Sister Anna says . . . go to bed alone. Tomorrow I shall meet you when you come off duty, and we shall decide about Canada."

"You must go if your work takes you there, Rob. It's too good an opportunity to miss."

"You must come, Anna. Tomorrow I shall ask you again and you will say yes. I shall buy you a ring . . . I've never bought an engagement ring for a woman before. That shows that I love you." Anna helped him to his feet, as the deep chair was low and even now he was not in full control of his limbs.

"Goodnight, Rob," she said determinedly. His grip on her arm tightened. "You must go; even if I don't come with you, you should take this job." She shook her head as he tried to speak. "I can't make up my mind tonight. I'm almost as confused as you are. Please, Rob, wait. If I am coming with you, I'll be at the lodge at nine tomorrow night. I have to think. It means the end of Beattie's for me, and that means a lot. If I come, we shall have to be married before we leave and it will be for keeps, but I have to consider everything. I'm too influenced by having you near to me, and I have to be objective."

86

She could not recognise herself in this woman. Anna of two years ago would have flung herself into his arms and given her promise at once. Had two years made her cautious? Or was she a different person?

"If you loved me as I love you, there would be no need to think it over," he said, echoing her own thoughts.

"I have a deep hurt to consider," she answered. "When you left I thought I would die, but I've lived, as so many live, although my heart was dented in places. You must give me until tomorrow to make up my mind, Rob. Goodnight."

He put his arms round her, and for the first time she saw in his eyes the expression that two years ago she would have given anything to see. It was the look of a man totally in love, and with desire there was tenderness.

If only, she thought, and as his lips came down on her trembling mouth, she wondered why she had wavered. In spite of all his faults, he was Rob, the man who could make her helpless with one kiss.

She broke away, stiffening as his hands began to wander over her breasts and wondered why she was faintly repelled in spite of her first reaction. It was the smell of whiskey, she thought. Tomorrow he would be fine.

A movement from the doorway made her pull away from Rob and swing round. Slade was standing there, his face expressionless. "Sorry to break it up," he said, "but Sir Horace needs you to assist him. This is a private case and it's urgent."

CHAPTER FIVE

THE smell of the theatre and the faint hum of the air filters seemed unreal in the silence. Anna hurried to her office where the light shone and vague figures could be seen through the frosted glass panel.

"Ah, there you are, my dear." Sir Horace looked tired. "I should be on my way to Birmingham for the conference tomorrow, but I couldn't leave one of our own people to other hands, especially as she asked for me."

Anna stared at him. Slade had not mentioned anything about the patient being a member of the staff of Beattie's.

"Didn't you know? I thought you knew her. She isn't with us now, of course, not on the staff . . . flattered to think she remembered us . . . married some wealthy foreigner or other, didn't she?" He went towards the theatre and Anna heard the sound of the lift. "I sent for her. She's in the private wing as there are no spare beds here. Should be up in ten minutes. Does that give you time?"

Anna nodded. "Yes, Sir Horace. Mr. Forsythe told me you'd need a general set and a few extras. Acute abdomen, isn't it? There's an emergency drum sterile with all you should need for that, and I've asked Night Sister for an extra nurse to check swabs." She saw that Slade had joined them and wondered why he looked so pale. So, it would be Sir Horace, Slade Forsythe and she would be scrubbing, with one anaesthetic nurse and one runner, and the anaesthetist. She quickly checked the anaesthetic room and sterilisers and made sure that the nurse sent by Night Sister knew what was required of her, then joined the two men at the scrubbing bay.

"I know you feel concerned, Forsythe," said Sir Horace. "Known her for a long time, haven't you? Thought at one time that you and she . . . ? None of my business, but my wife likes to ferret out all the gossip, you know."

He laughed, but Slade Forsythe continued to scrub his hands, his eyes hidden by the shadow of the green linen theatre cap. Anna busied herself with the trolley, counting packs of dressings and swabs, threading needles and laying ampoules of catgut ready for breaking as they would be needed.

The instruments were laid in neat groups, the sterile towels ready to unfold, and at last she could tear her thoughts away from the important work of preparation. He had said that the patient had been on the staff . . . had married a foreigner. Anna felt cold with apprehension. It couldn't be . . . it wasn't possible . . . Carmel, the girl who had taken Rob from her and nearly broken her heart, was in South America! Slade had said nothing when he gave her the message from Sir Horace. In fact, he had turned away and gone as soon as he was sure that Anna was going back to the theatre, as if he couldn't get away fast enough.

She listened, and from further remarks from the surgeon she was left in no doubt that the patient who would be wheeled in from the anaesthetic room would be Carmel. Was that why Slade looked so pale? Did her presence mean something to him after all? He hadn't mentioned her name in front of Rob, and that could mean one of many things. He could be sparing Rob's feelings in the belief that Carmel might once more have some influence over him . . . or it would prevent Rob from deserting Anna a second time.

Her cheeks flamed under the mercifully concealing mask. When Slade burst in on them, it must have seemed that she and Rob were together again for keeps. She glanced at his still, tall figure but could not read in his face or attitude anything but the alert readiness of the dedicated doctor waiting for his patient.

The lights shone down on to the table and the double doors slid back to let the trolley come into the room. The porter and nurse helped the anaesthetist to lift the still form on to the operating table and the nurse drew back the covering sheet.

Carmel, even in a baggy theatre gown, had beauty. Unconscious, she lacked movement, the restless, cat-like movement that stirred men and made even women look at her, but even so she retained her beauty in the fine curves of her splendid body and the classic sculpture of her lovely profile. Her skin was sunburned and hid the pallor of her face, making it seem impossible that there was anything wrong with her. Sir Horace raised his eyebrows, and the anaesthetist nodded and sat on his stool at the head of the table, checking the monitor and the cylinders.

Anna draped the bare abdomen with sterile towels, handing sterile towel clips to Slade Forsythe to secure the linen in a neat square exposing the flat smooth flesh. Sir Horace raised his scalpel and a moment later, Anna was too busy to think who it was under the knife. The outer layers of tissue were separated, swabbed and the bleeding points sealed with a diathermy needle. Sir

Horace put a gentle exploratory finger into the cavity and grunted.

"Thought so. Difficult to tell from her symptoms if it was an appendix or an ovary, but I was pretty sure. Here, Forsythe . . . feel this."

The other man examined the swelling exposed and Anna handed warm saline towels to pack at the edges of the wound before inserting the self-retaining retractor. "Ovarian cyst . . . quite innocent, but it would have given her a lot of trouble." All the time, the thin blade and gentle pressure of a swab-covered gloved finger pushed away the angry-looking adhesions that had formed over the inflamed area. It was obvious that the condition had been there for some time, but giving no more than a niggling discomfort until recently.

The cyst was removed and the raw area on the ovary exposed. Sir Horace hesitated. "What do you think, Slade?" he said.

"I think that she would be very grateful if you could make sure that as few adhesions form as possible, Sir. She has married into a family who will expect her to have children . . . an heir is important. Ovulation will be painful if we leave it like that . . . at least for a time."

Sir Horace grunted, and Anna passed the inner sterile envelope containing the thin membrane that she knew would be needed. Carefully, it was spread over the inflamed area of the ovary like a patch to protect it from the surrounding tissue and so prevent it sticking to any other organ. It was a pet procedure of Beattie's men, used by Sir Horace many times in cases such as this one. Slade began to take out the saline packs and Anna checked swabs with the runner. Sir Horace announced that the appendix was blameless and closed

91

the wound with swift skill. He ran an invisible line of fine catgut under the skin, bringing the skin edges together neatly. He patted the line with an antiseptic swab and smiled. "That's why she wanted you, Sir," said Slade, with a trace of humour in his voice for the first time.

"Cheeky young rascal! She wanted me because she knew I'd make a good job where it matters . . . under that scar." Sir Horace laughed. "But you're right . . . these vain females think more about their bikinis than their insides, and I *do* sew a fine seam, eh, Sister?"

Anna smiled and told the nurse to put coffee in the surgeons' room. Sir Horace peeled off his gloves and sighed. "I'll have a quick cup of coffee, and if you'd ring down for my car, I'll be on my way. If I'm to be coherent at the conference, I'll have to have a nap in the car." He looked at Slade, who was helping the porter to lift Carmel on to the trolley. "D'you mind, Slade?"

Slade Forsythe shook his head and assured Sir Horace that he would see to everything. "Perhaps you'd pop in and see her on your way back to the hurses' home, Sister. My chauffeur is bringing some flowers from my wife. Ah . . . there he is."

Anna took the bouquet of flowers and placed them in her office. When she went back to the theatre, the two men had gone, the anaesthetic room door was wide open and a trail of theatre-green clothes lay across the floor of the surgeons' room. Was it possible that it had really been Carmel in the theatre?

The theatre was soon restored to its usual gleaming calm, poised ready for use, emergency drums on the side rails and the autoclave spitting gently as the used and re-packed drums were sterilised. The night staff promised to turn off the autoclave when it was ready and Anna realised for the first time that she was wearing ordinary clothes under her theatre garb. She slipped out of the rubber boots and put on her dainty shoes and clicked off the light in her office.

The flowers lay in their plastic film. Sir Horace or his wife must have ordered them from Michael. They must send flowers where other people could only afford to send a card or a note, she thought, and remembered the red roses that she believed had come from Rob Delaney.

The corridor outside the private patients' wing was dimly lit and the thick carpet dulled her footsteps as Anna went along the row of doors. At number five, she stopped and a nurse who was passing smiled as she recognised the new sister in mufti.

"Shall I give these to you?" asked Anna. "No . . . I'll take them in. You're busy. I'll put them in the sink with some water and you can arrange them when you have time."

Curiosity drew her to the side of the woman who had once hurt her so deeply. The outer door was slightly ajar; all private rooms had two doors to insulate the rooms against noise, but when a patient was very ill or recovering from an anaesthetic, the outer door was left open so that any sound from the patient could be heard. The space between the doors was flanked by a simple but spacious wardrobe, a contrast to the limited space allowed ward patients. On the wardrobe door hung the clothes that Carmel had worn to the hospital.

A faint scent, so subtle that it must have been very expensive, so different from the smell of the theatre that Anna had left a few minutes earlier, came from the clothes. Anna put out a hand and touched the dress. In the dim light it looked like dull velvet or matt silk, but her fingers encountered the softness of beautifully worked suede. The cut of the deceptively simple garment was faultless, the finish only to be obtained from the finest of *haute couture* and the elegance unmistakable.

The clothes that Anna wore suddenly seemed shabby and quite uninteresting. Her pretty shoes cheap beside the suede high-heeled sandals that so perfectly matched the dress and which could be seen peeping out of the alcove reserved for shoes. Carmel had everything . . . beauty, a dynamic personality, clothes and a wealthy husband.

Why did she have to come back? Anna clenched her hands and nearly dropped the flowers. Why should this woman return to disrupt her life again? She would mean trouble wherever there were other women . . . wherever there were handsome and impressionable men. It wasn't fair. Anna was tired . . . so tired that she had that false sense of over-brightness that sometimes comes with fatigue.

She pushed open the inner door and stood unobserved, the scene before her etching itself on her brittle mind. A murmur of voices hid the small gasp that came from the woman in the doorway.

Anna could not move forward and she dared not risk leaving before she had left the flowers. The night nurse in the corridor would think her mad if she came out still carrying them. She held the flowers tightly and the murmuring voices stopped. Slade Forsythe glanced up from his place by the bedside and the light from the shaded lamp shone on the softly curving arms that he gently disentangled from around his neck. Carmel lay flat, her dark hair free from the restriction of the theatre cap, her throat and bosom edged by delicate silk that looked dusky and warm in the muted light.

"Sir Horace asked me to leave these flowers," Anna said stiffly. "I'll put them in the sink with some water and leave you . . . in peace."

Slade sat up, his face flushed with embarrassment. The half-drugged woman on the bed groped for him, missing the strong arms that had held her.

"Slade . . . Slade, darling. Don't leave me . . . you are the one . . . the one . . . one."

Her voice trailed away as she slipped into a natural sleep. Anna's face was set in a falsely polite smile. She walked quickly across to the hand basin and took the film from the flowers. The water was cold on her hot wrist as she spread the stems to let them drink, and she tried to ignore the man who now stood by the bedside, adjusting his tie.

"Sister . . . Anna . . . I was just making sure that Carmel was comfortable."

"There is no need to explain, Mr. Forsythe. I heard Sir Horace turn his patient into your care . . . he would be so pleased to see you taking your duties so seriously." Her icy voice surprised even herself and Slade's face darkened with something more than mere embarrassment. "I quite understand how you must feel. It must have been a strain scrubbing up for someone you know so well. It is quite clear that you are . . . very fond of her and she of you."

She crumpled the wet plastic film into a ball and threw it into the waste basket. A murmur from the bed made her turn. Carmel held her arms out, as if to a lover. Her eyes were shut and she was obviously asleep,

95

but to Anna, it looked as if she wanted Slade to come back to her, to let her entwine her arms and her spell round him again. So it would be if she stayed . . . with Slade and Rob and any man who caught her eye.

Unshed tears stung Anna's eyelids as she swept from the room, ignoring the movement that Slade made to come to her. She failed to see the pain in his eyes and the disconsolate droop of his shoulders when she left but saw only the feline charmer on the bed . . . waiting . . . waiting.

"Everything all right, Sister?" The night nurse drew back as Anna stormed out of the private patients' wing.

"Yes, everything. It couldn't be better," snapped Anna, but back in her room she flung herself on the bed and the tears began to flow, painfully and in great gulping sobs.

As the first tide of emotion ebbed, she drank some cold water and tried to control her violent hiccoughs. She wondered for whom she was crying. Was it because she feared to lose Rob again? It was true that when he had kissed her, some of the old tremulous thrill had returned, and at that moment he had been the old Rob of her dreams and she the girl in love for the first time.

She sat on the edge of her bed, brushing her hair and hoping that the aspirin she had taken would deal with the headache caused by her weeping. If not Rob, then who? Carmel had no power to hurt her if she decided after all that Rob and Canada were not for her. Slade, then? He had known Carmel for years . . . had she been too hasty? Would not any man, a friend or a brother, have soothed a woman just coming out of painful unconsciousness?

Thinking back, Anna realised, it was Carmel who

had held Slade tightly in her arms. A slight smile twitched at the corner of her mouth. A human octopus! He really hadn't had a chance to escape without hurting the patient! And at Beattie's, the patient must be considered at all times!

Deeply ashamed at her outburst, and quite unable to remember what she had said to Slade, she knew that she had been very caustic and wounding. If he was in love with Carmel, then the cap fitted . . . he was overstepping the bounds of doctor-patient manners. But if he was merely comforting a miserable patient, gentling her into sleep with no feelings of desire, then Anna had made a terrible mistake, and she knew that it did matter.

She undressed and slipped into bed, lonely and weary. The light from the corridor outside shone through the transom on her door and she heard soft footsteps that paused at her door. Had he listened before he went on to his own room? Was he furious with her? Anna pulled the bedclothes high over her ears like a naughty child and fell asleep.

At breakfast, the trained staff were buzzing with the news that Carmel, the girl who had run away with Dr. Delaney, had come back to Beattie's for an operation. Rumours were flying when Anna listlessly helped herself to coffee and scrambled eggs.

"Who took theatre last night?" someone asked. Susan shook her head. It had been two in the morning before she returned from seeing her fiancé. "Well, someone from day staff must have done . . . Sir Horace wouldn't tolerate an untrained staff, and there's no one on nights who could satisfy all his little whims."

"I took it," Anna said coolly. There was silence. She smiled ruefully. "Sir Horace asked me to take theatre, and it all went off very well. One acute abdomen . . . not an abortion as I heard mentioned when I came in; a straightforward ovarian cyst with adhesions." She sipped her coffee.

"Who assisted?"

"Mr. Forsythe," she answered and buttered some toast, sensing the growing curiosity.

"Was it Mr. Forsythe who brought her into Beattie's?" said the same persistent sister. Susan shot her a warning glance which was ignored. "They were . . . very good friends once, weren't they?"

A low murmur of amusement greeted her remarks and she was encouraged to further efforts. "I wonder who she is after this time. Seems strange that she should appear just when both the men she dated here are around again."

"She is married," said Anna, with an effort to sound disinterested. "She was on a shopping trip to London and was taken ill. Naturally, she wanted the very best treatment and came here to the hospital she knew and to Sir Horace, who she insisted was the only man she would trust to operate on her."

She buttered more toast. I'm beginning to convince myself, she thought. It was simple. It really could have happened like that. "I don't think she will be here for many days. Sir Horace said that some relatives of her husband want her to go to them and have a private nurse while she recovers."

She had forgotten that he had said it until this moment. Her spirits rose. Perhaps Carmel would go and never return, and Rob . . . would not be drawn back into her toils. But it didn't matter. If Rob wanted her, he would follow her. He had said he had finished with Carmel and now, in the light of a working day, Anna believed him. He had been sincere in his declaration of love, and it was only the lateness of the case and the weariness of her mind that had made her think any other way.

"I've got to get on duty," she said abruptly. The others watched her go and she knew that the moment the door closed behind her, a burst of gossip and speculation would buzz round the dining-room about her and Rob. Let them . . . what does it matter? she thought, and wandered along to the ward with none of the haste she had pretended. What does anything matter but work . . . and Beattie's, and friends?

"Lost a fortune and found a penny?" Susan's cheerful voice came from behind her. "Thought you were in a hurry."

"No . . . I felt it better to let them get it all said and have done with it. They *did* talk about . . . me and Rob, I suppose?"

"I stopped it. Silly cat! There's always one, isn't there? I told them that you'd make up your own mind and didn't need their help. I also told them that Slade Forsythe knew Carmel when they were children. She looks on him as some kind of a relative, and he promised to look after her when she came to Beattie's. I imagine he must have heaved a sigh of relief when she was safely married. Takes his duties seriously, does our Slade."

Anna recalled the arms about his neck and his acute embarrassment. "Doesn't he just," she said softly. "How do you know so much about him?"

"He told me," Sue told her complacently. "That's one of the perks of being a safely engaged female. Men like Slade respect it and talk to me. I feel a hundred, sometimes! He comes in to see me and I think he fancies me, and then he tells me about his mother and his brother and his friends!" She glanced at Anna. "And he uses me to find out about the staff here." Anna looked surprised. "Oh, yes, very curious he is about certain members," she added, with an expression that said 'I-know-something-that-you-don't-know.'

"Is that the time?" Anna sprinted along to her office, where the night staff waited ready to go off duty. Slade had asked questions? About whom? Did Susan know the identity of the woman he had hinted he loved? Was she still at Beattie's?

"I'm sorry, Nurse. You were saying?" But if he loved someone, surely he would have told her by now . . . and if he had, what girl could resist the appeal of those deep-set eyes?

"I'm sorry, you'll have to excuse me, I can't concentrate this morning," she said. "It was a busy night." There was a murmur of sympathy. "But there are no cases this morning, so I can take my time. Now, Nurse, how is Mrs. Brown?"

Report was finished and Anna gave her attention to the routine of the morning. She made her usual round of the patients and listened to a few grumbles and many expressions of gratitude. Gradually her tiredness left her, and she was fully involved with the recovery of her patients, their hopes and fears and touching confidence in the fact that the staff at Beattie's was the best in the world. She took time to sit with a woman who was worried because someone had told her that her husband would lose all interest in her after her hysterectomy. Anna explained that with none of her symptoms of bleeding, and no more of the anxiety they had shared that perhaps the condition was cancer and not the innocent fibroids found when the operation was performed, she would be more relaxed, feel clean and wholesome and therefore more attractive than she had been for a long time.

"I never thought of that, Sister. Oh, I wish I'd come in months ago! Looking back, I really was in a state. I used to cry and I lost all my colour. I had quite pretty rosy cheeks before the bleeding started."

Anna glanced at the chart and saw that the blood count was still low, and treatment had been written up for that morning.

"We're trying to bring back the roses," she smiled. "A nice young lady will come to give you some blood this morning. They took a specimen to cross-match last night, I believe." Roses, thought Anna. Roses in a woman's cheeks, roses in the garden . . . red roses in a vase.

"I was talking to two other women in Outpatients," said Mrs. Bale, "they told me the same, that they were frightened that their marriages would suffer. I wish you'd been there to tell them all you've told me, Sister. I know that one was terribly worried."

Anna made a mental note that this was one of the important duties of a sister, to ease the mind as well as the body, to give confidence and hope as well as good physical care. It was good to be wanted . . . needed . . . as Beattie's needed her. "Yes, Nurse, what is it?" she said to the junior hovering at a distance from the bed-curtain.

"Sister, Mr. Forsythe wants to do a round."

"He's very early. Sir Horace doesn't usually come until the ward is clear."

"He apologised, Sister, but he said he had to see Sir Horace's private patients as well as his own on the wards. He's lecturing the final year nurses at ten-thirty."

Anna adjusted the bow under her chin and glanced in the mirror. She saw a slim girl in a slightly old-fashioned uniform of great charm and dignity . . . at least, that was the reflection in the mirror. But what registered with her was a skirt too long for fashion, a dull colour and a feeling of general dowdiness. The crisp cotton did not resemble, in texture or appearance, the soft fall of the fine suede she had seen the night before. She caught a whiff of Dettol as she passed the sluice room. Hardly Chanel Number Five!

Slade Forsythe greeted her with professional courtesy, apologising once more for the early start. Anna just nodded and picked up the notes from the first bed and gave a report on the patient's condition. There was a cool air between them as they went from bed to bed, but none of the patients seemed to notice any tension. Slade was gentle and attentive, listening gravely to complaints of discomfort and smiling at good progress. How good he is at his job, Anna thought reluctantly.

A young girl, being investigated for a hormone deficiency, greeted him ecstatically. She showed him the gifts brought in by her parents, and as he bent to examine a particularly luridly coloured get-well card, she impulsively put an arm round him and hugged him.

"That's enough, young lady," he said, smiling. "Put me down at once, or Sister will imagine all kinds of things." He straightened. "The hazards of my profession, Sister." He gave a slight and very mocking bow, and his smile was only on his lips.

"You manage the . . . hazards very well, Mr. Forsythe." She picked up the next set of X-rays. "But then, of course, you must have lots of experience of such situations."

The air seemed to tremble between them before it became a barrier of thin ice. He's very angry with me, she thought, and knew that her attempt to hide her humiliation was making her sound bitchy. They finished the round quickly. Slade made brief notes, using a bed-table and not entering her office, before nodding curtly and rushing away.

"If I'm needed, I shall be in P.P. wing for half an hour and then in the lecture room," he told her.

"Give my regards to Carmel," said Anna, unable to stop herself. "I hope that she has everything she requires."

He looked at her with something approaching dislike in his eyes. "I shall give her no such message. If you really wish her well, go and see her. I pass on no messages that aren't sincere." He went before she could reply and only the fact that the whole ward could see her gave Anna the strength to pick up the notes he had consulted and put them away again.

How he must despise her, she thought. How childish her behaviour must seem, and how annoying for him to have a woman in whom he had only a workaday interest hinting that he was unprofessional! She recalled the buzz of gossip at breakfast. He was wise and very, very clever to keep the identity of the woman he loved . . . if it wasn't Carmel . . . away from those prying minds.

She opened the theatre records and checked that all the details were correct for the last list. She was making too much of Slade's reaction. If he thought of her as just a Sister running the ward and theatre where he worked, he would take no notice of odd moods and put down her rudeness to her being over-tired. After all, it was usually surgeons who had the reputation of being edgy after long hours on duty, so why not Sisters as well?

Sir Horace rang from Birmingham. "How is my prize patient?" He sounded jocular, and Anna guessed that the conference was going well.

"I hear that she is sitting up and all is well, sir," said Anna.

"You hear? Haven't you seen for yourself?"

"I went last night and took the flowers. She had Mr. Forsythe there, and this morning I haven't had time to go across." It sounded very ungracious to her as she said it. What had Slade said? 'If you wish her well, go and see her.'

"Well, I hope you make time," said Sir Horace, a trifle testily. "Poor child, she's lonely. Her husband is in America and her family away. She faces the thought of convalescing in a gloomy country house with her husband's aged uncle and aunt, who have lived in this country for years, but still treat their women as if they need to be locked up." He chuckled. "They obviously think she's less likely to run off with a handsome doctor if she is well chaperoned, eh, Sister?" He coughed. "Know it must be difficult for you, m'dear. I believe I put my great feet in it the other day. I hope all goes well with young Delaney and you. Carmel was spoiled . . . always spoiled, but she means no harm. Go and say hello and give her my love."

104

Anna put down the phone and sighed. Kittens didn't mean to scratch, either . . . means no harm, indeed! But she resolved to see Carmel as soon as she went off duty . . . no, she'd pop in at lunch-time, in uniform.

Ruefully, she admitted to herself that she could not visit the other woman dressed in her off-duty clothes. The thought of the suede dress was still with her. Uniform would be at once formal and in no way in competition. Before she went to lunch she was called to the outside telephone again.

"Rob! I told you not to ring me on duty."

"I hear that my favourite vampire is with you." His voice was cold, as if it were her fault that Carmel had re-appeared. "I shall keep clear. If I were to see that woman again, I think I'd do her an injury. If she asks about me, tell her to go to Hell."

"I never pass on loving messages," Anna said, and smiled slightly, thinking she must have sounded to Slade as Rob now sounded to her.

"Don't you mind that she's here? Aren't you jealous? Don't you know that she wouldn't come unless she wanted something? Me, for instance?"

Anna knew with sudden clarity that she was jealous . . . but not of Carmel and Rob. She envied Carmel her clothes, the ease with which she had requested Sir Horace for her operation and her influence over Slade Forsythe.

"She did come because she wanted something, Rob, but she doesn't want you. She wanted a firm assurance that she can have children. She is married now, and I believe is sincere in the fact that she wants to give her husband an heir. Can't you see her once, to wish her well?"

"I tell you, Anna, I never want to hear her name again. I shall keep away from P.P. until she's gone, so let's forget she ever existed." The bitterness in his voice made her wince. "I mean it, Anna. I never want you to mention her name to me again."

"You may be right," said Anna, crisply, "but I can't stay on this line. Must go . . . I have to see a patient."

The private patients' wing was bathed in sunlight. The antique furniture in the foyer gleamed softly with the gentle polish of years, and the fresh flowers on the brass tray reflected back their own glow. This was a part of the old building, and someone had been far-sighted enough to keep the best of the old to combine harmoniously with the latest in comfort and safety. The dress was no longer on the hanger by Carmel's door, and everything was neatly put away. The flowers from Sir Horace were arranged in a crystal vase and another smaller spray of cream roses lay in a shallow blue bowl.

"Hello," said Anna, "what lovely flowers." I sound like a stranger, she thought, visiting a ward as my good deed for the day.

"Anna Boswell?" Carmel looked paler this morning. Her eyes lacked the fire that Anna recalled from the days when she undulated round the hospital as a physiotherapist, making all heads turn. "They told me you brought Sir Horace's flowers and that you stayed late for me in the theatre. It was good of you." Her voice was curiously flat.

"I'm sorry that you had this trouble," replied Anna.

"Are you?" For a moment, the tawny spark was there. "I would have thought you would be glad." She shut her eyes as if to shut out her own thoughts. "I wish I'd never come here. I had a long telephone call from my husband who says I must go to his uncle. He does not trust me here. Someone told him about . . . many things."

"About you and Rob living together?" Anna was cool.

"That and other matters." She sighed. "None of it was important . . . it was amusing. And now, my old, dear friend, Slade . . . he is not kind any more. He has told me of my sins and makes me promise to be a good wife and bear many children." She flicked the bed cover with a petulant hand. "It will be so boring."

A flicker of a smile came to Anna's lips. She was no longer jealous of this beautiful woman. What did it matter if she had lovely clothes, expensive cars and a bevy of servants to come when she wanted the slightest thing? She had lost the one thing that mattered to the kittens of the world. She had been caged, and she could no longer roam and find adventure where she wished, could no longer sample the pleasures of illicit love. Poor Carmel, thought Anna, and was sorry for her.

"I shall be fat and ugly when I am pregnant." She glanced at Anna's trim figure. "Women like you need never fear that . . . I wish I had inherited that part of my English ancestors! I have inherited a love of freedom and a tendency to fat!"

Anna laughed. "You are just suffering from post-surgical depression. Come on, Carmel, you don't mean half of what you say and I believe that once you have made up your mind to enjoy motherhood, you will be superb." What could Carmel ever be in whatever role she cast herself, but superb? "Just think how lovely your children will be with fine dark eyes and dark brown hair."

"Yes . . ." Carmel thought about it. "I might find it amusing, and children do not stay as children for ever. I shall do my duty, and then who knows . . . I shall still be young."

She smiled and touched a petal of one of the pale roses. "I wish that Slade had given me red roses instead of these." She looked at Anna. "He told me to be glad he had brought me any at all. He has become very strict, that one. He said that he only gave red roses to people who deserved them. He said they were for love." She sighed. "Darling Slade . . . so English, but so very good."

"But these are lovely," said Anna, bending over the sweet-smelling flowers.

"My children will never have English roses in their cheeks. When you have children, they will be pink and white and have skins like silk. Do you know how much I envy you that, Sister Anna Boswell?" Carmel's tone was light and mocking but her eyes were sad and for the first time, Anna realised how much Carmel was torn between her two races. In England it was good to have the reputation of being Latin and exotic, but in South America, would she not miss everything she had taken for granted . . . freedom of women, green fields and an interesting job?

"I hope that you are very happy. I'm sure you will be if you accept certain limitations. At least you will have wonderful horses to ride. You love riding, don't you?"

Carmel nodded. "You are very generous, Anna. I shall remember that you wished me well. Go now, please." Her eyes filled with tears, and Anna left quickly to save her pride.

She stopped at the door of the office of the sister in

charge of private patients and looked in. "Is Sir Horace's patient all right?" Sister Smythe came out into the corridor. "It's probably nothing, but she seemed very depressed."

Anna frowned. It wasn't even depression that had made her uneasy. "Maybe I'm imagining it, but I had the feeling that everything wasn't quite right."

"I'm glad you came in," said Sister Smythe. "I had the same feeling. It's nothing I could pin down, but her eyes look dull, and although her respirations are regular and her pulse as you would expect after an acute abdomen, I thought her breathing was shallow." She looked at her watch. "Mr. Forsythe said he'd come back to see her. She was sound asleep when he looked in." She went along the corridor. "I think I'll bleep him. Was she very inflamed?"

Anna nodded. "Lots of very nasty adhesions, and the fallopian tube was stuck down. Could be infected."

Sister Smythe called a nurse. "Did you save the pad from Mrs. Gonzalez? Good, I'll come and inspect it." They went along to the bright chrome and white sluice room and the nurse raised the plastic sheet covering the tray of vaginal pads. The one from Carmel was stained with a little dark blood and little more, but a thin ring of serious discharge surrounded the stain.

"Get the house surgeon to write up a path. form and take it along, Nurse. It may be quite all right, but we can't be sure." The internal telephone rang. "Oh, Mr. Forsythe. Sorry to bother you but you still have to examine Mrs. Gonzalez. She's awake, and I would like you to see her." She put down the receiver. "He's coming at once."

"I'll go," said Anna, "I was on my way to lunch."

Suddenly she wanted to get away before Slade appeared. It's no business of his, she thought, I am only doing what Sir Horace asked me to do; it has nothing to do with what Slade had said in the cold, reproving voice. Sir Horace had asked her to visit his patient and she had done so, delivered his messages and . . . wished her well. But the well-wishing had not been a message from Sir Horace, had it?

"I beg your pardon." Anna clutched at her cap as she nearly lost her footing. Slade Forsythe was holding her to stop her falling, looking down with a comical expression of surprise on his face. He held her tightly for long moments after she was quite safe and seemed to forget to release her.

His concern held something that made Anna veil her eyes with her long eyelashes and break away, rubbing her ankle vigorously so that he wouldn't see her blush. "Did I hurt you?" He was coming towards her again and she retreated. "I hardly thought I'd bump into you here," he said, as she shook off his offer of help.

"I'm fine. Just caught my ankle, but even the stocking is still intact," Anna replied. He stared gravely at the slim foot she displayed and she blushed again. "I'll be late for lunch," she said, and fled, but had the feeling that two grey eyes watched her go along the corridor and out through the swing doors.

"Where did you get to?" said Susan. "Your staff nurse said you'd left for lunch early as you had to go somewhere on your way."

"I called in at P.P.," said Anna.

"Well, I must say, you're a devil for punishment! Not visiting old enemies now, are we?"

Anna helped herself to cauliflower. "Sir Horace rang

110

and asked me to go over to see Carmel. He said she was fed up and far from home, or words to that effect."

"What? No band of handsome men to hold her hand?"

Anna smiled. "Do you know, Sue, I used to hate her so much that I thought I could kill her. I thought she was thoroughly bad and amoral."

"And one visit to our theatre has purged her of all wickedness?"

"No, she's still the same old Carmel, but I no longer envy her. She has everything that money can buy, but she is kept on a very tight rein. I saw the photograph of her husband. He's very good-looking; a strong face and rather bull-like body. Handsome and right for Carmel, but he'll stand no nonsense from her. I believe she's met a man who can dominate her."

She laughed and told Susan that Carmel was doomed to stay with the strict relatives. "I think that's what's making her so depressed." She frowned. "But it wasn't just that," she said, almost to herself.

Sister Smythe bustled into the sitting-room where Anna was having after-lunch coffee with three other Sisters.

"Ah, there you are, Boswell. Thought you'd like to know that Mrs. Gonzalez is all right." She accepted the cup of coffee and sat on the arm of a chair. "I can't stop. I was late for lunch, but I must get back."

"What happened?"

"Mr. Forsythe came. Just after you left, actually. Wonder you didn't bump into him." Anna smiled. "He examined her and read the riot act. She hasn't been drinking enough, she slumps down in bed and doesn't breathe properly, and she seems to be making no effort

111

to get better. Besides which, she now says she is allergic to the antibiotic they started last night. No wonder she feels off-colour! It's enough to have an operation and the post-surgical pain without adding to it." She put down her cup. "I suppose it didn't occur to her to tell anyone that she was allergic?" Anna shook her head. "No, I thought not. She only discovered it seven months ago when she tore a muscle on her leg which discharged badly. Caught it on a tree-stump, she said. The doctor in South America gave her the same drug and she was quite ill."

She put the cup back on the tray and smiled. "Just as well you came to see her. I must confess that I would have given her the two o'clock dose without a second thought, but as soon as Mr. Forsythe saw her and asked her a few questions, he cancelled the prescription and wrote her up for something different. Between us, we might have saved her a lot of trouble." She hurried away and Anna sensed the interest of the others.

"Just as well that Sir Horace asked you to check," said Susan pointedly, making it clear that the visit was a duty one. "She'll be well enough to go to her doting relatives with a private nurse tomorrow, after all!" She grinned. "Poor Carmel, she might have preferred a little discomfort here." She glanced at Anna. "Not that I would wish that on her – nasty things, allergies. What a good thing you went along when you did, Anna!"

"They would have guessed something was wrong as soon as Mr. Forsythe came," said Anna.

"But they might have given her the next dose if Sister Smythe hadn't bleeped him. She said that she thought she'd let the poor man have lunch before bothering him, and then when you said you weren't too happy

112

about Carmel, she rang early. He wouldn't have gone to see her until long after the two o'clock dose unless she had done so."

"He might have looked in," said Anna. "No one can accuse him of neglecting patients."

"No, that's the last thing he'd do, but a highly trained sister is his first line of defence against unnecessary calls on his time. If Smythe had missed it, it would have been his responsibility even though it wasn't his fault."

"Well, I hope that Smythe takes the credit. I just don't want to be involved," Anna said firmly. "I don't think that Mr. Forsythe approves of me very much."

"You should be pleased to think he might be impressed by your expertise," declared Susan.

"No," Anna contradicted firmly, and she had a sneaking feeling that his approval would be more than she could bear. She recalled the strong arms that had held her as she staggered and the genuine concern in those grey eyes. She distrusted her own reaction, and she felt that for her own peace of mind, the less she saw of him the better it would be.

"I was saying, before you went into orbit, that I had tickets for *Evita*," said Susan.

"Sorry," said Anna, "I was thinking of something I had to do."

She made her escape and went back to the nurses' home to collect her mail. There was a note from Rob reminding her that he intended seeing her and really talking. It was almost a threat. She turned to letters from home, and decided it was high time she visited her parents. It was strange that they seemed so far away. Every time she saw them, she wished she could stay

113

longer, but when she left, it was as if the train broke a tightly stretched ribbon between them, making a gulf over which they could not reach her. Beattie's was its own world and increasingly, she was a part of that world. Could parents, or Rob, or any man take her away from it?

But a niggling doubt crept into her thoughts. What of the future? Although she no longer envied Carmel, it was a fact that Carmel would have everything that Anna would never know if she remained at Beattie's and did not marry. Carmel had said that English children had pink and white skins . . . like roses. Anna looked up at the austere strength of the old block. Beattie's would take her life and service, given gladly, but would it be enough? Would she never long to let herself droop a little, to be held when tired and comforted by strong masculine arms? Hold her own child in her arms instead of soothing other people's sick children?

She saw Slade hurrying to the pathological department, and she turned away so that he would not see her.

CHAPTER SIX

THE ward telephone seemed to ring endlessly, and Anna found it difficult to make a full round of the ward. She had come on duty in time to relieve her staff nurse for lunch and the rest of the busy day lay ahead, with two new admissions, two cases of some urgency to be dealt with in the theatre and a grateful and rather tearful patient to see who had left the unit on the second day after the opening. She came to tell Anna that the biopsy had been innocent and that she no longer dreaded the possibility that she might have a growth on the lip of her womb.

Anna was as pleased as she was, and hastened to say that although she would receive a letter asking her to come to Outpatients soon, it would be for a check to make sure that everything had healed and not that they had discovered anything fresh in tissue sent for culture. The fact that she could have a normal married life was obviously of great importance to the patient.

"My husband began to look at other girls, Sister. We began to have such rows over it, but I know he'd rather have me. That nice young man who did me said that we can get back to normal in three weeks." She sighed. "I'm going to buy a nice nylon nightie, Sister. It's going to be a second honeymoon, and it's all due to you here, and that nice young man, Dr. Forsythe."

Anna smiled and managed to escape. Gratitude was one thing, but to be held jointly responsible with Slade for the purchase of the nylon nightie was a bit much!

She paused to look at Sandra's chart. The temperature was niggling just above normal, but it was hardly surprising after the infection she had concealed in her right ovary which antibiotics could not cure without surgery. Anna examined her abdomen and found it softer than it had been when she felt it two days earlier. She smiled.

"Keep doing the exercises and you'll drain all that nasty stuff that's keeping your temperature up a little. Drink lots of water and fruit squash . . . you have far too much in that jug. Come on, drink another glass while I'm here."

"Sister, it's coming out of my ears," wailed Sandra.

"No, it isn't. From the amount on your chart, you've drunk very little since yesterday."

She stood by while Sandra gulped down some brightly-coloured liquid that Anna was sure had never met an orange, but seemed to be the one brand that husbands could find in the local shops. Anna went along the line and drew back curtains that were not needed, making the ward friendly and light. Behind one set of drawn curtains she could hear a low panting sound, and went to check what was happening. The house surgeon was listening for the heartbeat of the foetus, and the woman in the bed was trying to control her gasps so that he could hear. Fresh blood stained the sheets, and the girl was in pain. Anna beckoned the young doctor and he followed her outside.

"Bleep whoever is on emergencies," she said. "Can't you see she's in a bad way? She's losing the baby and needs to be in the theatre. It looks rather as if it's older than it says on the chart, and that might mean trouble."

He tried to say something, looking rather resentful. "Sorry to interfere," she apologised, "but I've seen that before. She's losing blood and having violent contractions. I'd say it was inevitable."

"You're right, of course, Sister." He took a deep breath. "Back to Sir Horace. I'll go and put on sackcloth and humble myself yet again at the feet of the great man."

Anna smiled, briefly, and went back to the patient, encouraging her to breathe through her mouth and pant when the contractions came. She told her, gently, that she must go to the operating theatre and called a nurse to prepare her. "I'm afraid it looks as if you'll lose the baby. Is it your first?"

"First and last if I have any choice! I got caught this time, but I'll know better in future."

She had no ring on her hands, and Anna felt a mixture of compassion and repugnance. In the notes was a query. Had the abortion been induced by a dirty instrument, or was it accidental? The curve on the chart showed a steady rise in pulse-rate and Anna was alarmed.

Sir Horace came quickly and took in the situation at a glance. "You were right to send for me," he said to the H.S., who had the grace to give Anna a glance of thanks. He ordered an injection to calm the patient then looked at the chart. "Um! I don't like it, Sister. I don't like it at all. If she has been messing around with knitting needles, and they still do it! Can't think why when it's a legal procedure in the right hands, but they still do it . . . and *that is* illegal," he said to his subordinate. "If she has interfered with the pregnancy, she has infected herself and we can't afford to introduce further infection. We must draw out the foetus and not push instruments or canulae inside the uterus. I think she's

117

too far on for a vacuum method. The placenta is formed and we must induce her by natural methods, or we'll have a roaring infection plus a haemorrhage if the placenta doesn't peel off cleanly."

He walked into the surgeons' room, smiling. "I'm going to do what I haven't done since I was a student. Ever heard of laminaria tents?"

"You mean the sticks of compressed Japanese sea-weed that are inserted into the neck of the womb to make it dilate and open? I've heard of them, but I didn't think they were used any more, sir," said the house surgeon.

"Not often, but there is still a place for them in cases like this, or when a woman is mentally ill and we want to handle her as little as possible. The stick of dry seaweed, sterilised, of course, swells gently and the uterus contracts as in normal labour."

"But she has been contracting, sir. She should deliver it without interference."

"You go and look at her, my lad! She stopped con-tracting and she's slowly bleeding. She has a state of inertia which means that if we don't get those contrac-tions going, fast, she will bleed badly."

Anna blessed the common sense that the older man showed, and made sure that everything was ready. A whiff or two of gas and air which Anna gave was sufficient anaesthetic, and in a very short while, the girl was back in bed, resting fairly peacefully while a nurse stayed close to record the frequency of the contractions. A course of antibiotics was begun, and Sir Horace was satisfied. He nodded affably as he left the ward, even smiling at his house surgeon, a definite improvement in his manner towards him.

The theatre was scrubbed and purified, the instruments sterilised and an aura of damp disinfectant pervaded the corridor. The evening came quickly, and Anna had to check the time twice because she couldn't believe that it was so late.

Susan looked in to the office on her way off duty and Anna gave out the evening drugs. Trolleys were cleared, lockers tidied and the day staff could imagine that they might after all, get off duty on time. Anna gathered them in the office, except for one nurse who was keeping an eye on the girl with the abortion, which had happened quietly and painlessly at five o'clock, leaving no complications behind. A full course of antibiotics should clear the infection and the girl would be one of the lucky ones who had no lasting bad effects. Anna gave report and took details for her own report to Matron's office, lectured on the care of threatened abortion and was closing her theatre ledger when the telephone rang.

The tiny circle of faces stared at her as she listened to the voice of Slade Forsythe. Her manner became attentive and crisp. "Right," she said, "we'll be ready, Mr. Forsythe." She looked at the expectant faces. "Nurse, go to the side ward and check the bed. See that it moves freely into all positions. It shouldn't need oiling, but make sure . . . never take it for granted that an item of equipment is going to work; check it! You may never meet this kind of case again during your training. Some doctors never deal with one, but only know about it in theory." She waited another half a minute until the nurse returned and said that everything was ready for an emergency.

"A woman becomes pregnant, but the fertilised egg

119

does not go down far enough. It settles and clings to the tube leading from the ovary to the uterus," Anna said quickly. They nodded. "As the baby grows, there is no room for it and the tube becomes tight and inflamed and sometimes bursts. The result is a sudden internal bleeding and the patient is deeply shocked." She stopped to listen but could hear no ambulance bell.

"Can we stay on duty, Sister?" said a very junior nurse.

Anna hesitated. "It will help nobody if you get in the way. Some of you have not worked in the theatre and if you came, you would see very little." She nodded to the third-year nurse and a girl who was due for theatre duty. "You two can put on gowns and masks and stand well back. If I ask you for something, get it, or say firmly that you don't know where it is. Never dither, and never, ever, get in the way of the surgeon or he will be quite justified in swearing at you."

She smiled, easing the tension. "And he will, you know, even if you don't deserve it!" She gave them their instructions and put out the necessary instruments for sterilising, and when Slade Forsythe glanced in, there was a well-ordered buzz of activity. He went to the office. "I think everything is ready, Mr. Forsythe," Anna told him.

"Fine," he said, "I think the ambulance is on its way. I'll send some blood for cross-matching and start her on plasma if she needs it."

"There's a drip and cutting-down instruments in the room," said Anna. He nodded his approval and asked if she had ever seen a ruptured ectopic. "Yes," she said, "and I'll never forget it! By the way, Mr. Forsythe, two nurses are going to watch, if you have no objection.

120

They have been told to stand back and are not theatre staff, so please don't expect them to know anything about the procedure."

"I have two students who are hoping to do gynae. They will come too, but I have told them the same. If they get in the way, I'll have their guts for garters."

He was completely professional, completely detached, but Anna knew that it was right to be so. In an emergency, there was no time for personal feelings. "You'll scrub for me, Sister? The H.S. can get the drip going and when I've seen the patient and made sure the G.P. was right in his diagnosis, I'll get ready."

"I'll have everything ready. Do you want anything not in the general set of instruments?"

"No . ... we might have to put in a drain, but I hope to close completely. If she isn't losing below we can keep her clean and avoid a possible peritonitis." His bleeper sounded, and he listened and made for the door. "She's on her way up," he said.

Anna gave more instructions and asked the staff nurse from the other ward to take over in the side ward until the night staff arrived. "I'd better scrub and get the needles and diathermy ready," she said. "You know the classic signs? Deep shock, pallor, and the patient feels as if she is floating or sinking down through the bed. That's if she is bleeding a lot. The H.S. will put up a drip and the anaesthetist has been alerted. The patient's abdomen will be rock-hard and tender if she's a genuine rupture of the fallopian tube."

"She will have to lose the baby?" someone asked.

"She will be only a few weeks pregnant, probably. The baby will not be a developed baby, but a foetus. Try to remember that, Nurse . . . . it couldn't live."

She scrubbed and gowned and pulled on the sterile rubber gloves, checking the instruments and trying to think if there was any piece of equipment that just might be useful. When the anaesthetist arrived, all was ready and Anna stood like a pale-green statue with her hands held high to avoid contamination. A doctor stood by her, gowned and masked as she was, and he asked her questions, having never seen an ectopic. Only the dull hum of the air conditioning made a sound until trolley-wheels came along the corridor and the door to the side ward opened.

Moments later, Slade Forsythe strode into the theatre and began to scrub his hands vigorously. Everything swung into action as if rehearsed a hundred times. The patient was wheeled in, her feet high on the tilted trolley to relieve the pressure on her abdomen and to ensure a supply of blood to the brain. The drip was changed to blood as the cross-matched supply was rushed from the blood bank, the anaesthetist gently began to induce deep relaxation and light sleep and the area of her abdomen was swabbed and cleansed, surrounded by sterile towels and painted with mercurochrome, an antiseptic red dye that was a favourite preliminary of Slade's.

The lights shone down on the swathed figure, and the surgeon stood quite still, the scalpel poised for the first incision. It was a tableau that looked right, with everyone and everything in place and ready to go into action. A still life, awaiting a given signal. The anaesthetist nodded and Slade Forsythe shifted his feet slightly. He drew the blade across the taut, dyed skin and Anna handed him the first swab.

As the layers of tissue were exposed, separated, and

the bleeding points tied with fine catgut or sealed with a diathermy needle that burned the ends of small vessels that might ooze if left but were too small to tie off, Slade grunted.

"She left it a bit late," he said, "or someone did." The anaesthetist raised his eyebrows. "She's O.K.," said Slade, "but I've run into adhesions."

Anna passed him each instrument as he needed it, never having to be told which he wanted until it was time to close up the wound. Anna checked the used swabs and found that the total on the rack tallied with the count on the blackboard before handing him the first atraumatic needle, an eyeless needle that had catgut incorporated in it so that it would make only a fine hole in the tissues and not drag through a double thread and so tear the more delicate membrane.

Everyone breathed deeply; the drip was running well and the patient's colour, although pale, was not giving cause for alarm. Anna watched the long fingers tying knots, using scissors and gradually restoring all layers of muscle and membrane to their places. Slade worked swiftly, with a sure and delicate touch, and there was a certain beauty in the movements of his hands. Anna asked if he wanted a drain but he shook his head and asked for fine synthetic sutures for the skin.

"Why use those, sir?" asked one of the students. "Mr. Campbell uses thick nylon. He says they are easier to remove afterwards." There was a moment of silence as the entire theatre wondered what Mr. Forsythe would say. It was well-known that each surgeon had his own ideas, and some resented being compared to others. Slade finished the last of the skin sutures and patted the scar. The student seemed to think he had not heard and pushed his luck further. "Mr. Campbell . . ." he began.

"Look at that scar," said Slade. "I think it's beautiful!" He looked round the theatre. "Operations don't end here. This lady is pretty, quite young, and judging from her clothes when she was admitted, she likes to be in fashion." He glared at the unfortunate student. "If your girlfriend came here for this operation, would you want her to have a scar that will hardly show, like this, or have a ruddy great step-ladder from her pubis to her umbilicus?" He glanced at his house surgeon. "Make a note that she must buy a new bikini to show off her scar in Outpatients."

Everyone laughed, and the anaesthetist gave the order to ring for the theatre porter. The machines were turned off, the diathermy wheeled away to the side of the theatre and the emergency lights checked. The junior nurse swabbed the floor and the two nurses who had stayed on duty begged to be allowed to wash the instruments.

Their faces glowed with the kind of thrill that it is impossible to describe. A feeling of elation, of life preserved by skilled super-beings whom they could never hope to emulate but from whom they took a tiny scrap of glory just because they had been with them and seen for themselves.

Slade Forsythe peeled off his gloves and watched Anna giving quiet orders to her staff. She still wore gloves and mask, and the long gown trailed round her rubber boots. Aseptic, shapeless, disguised? Whoever said that shapeless gowns were without allure must be mad, he thought. He went into the surgeons' room to shower and change and was suddenly tired.

The patient was safely in bed in the side ward, and Anna was thankful that it was so near to the theatre from two points of view. It was good to be able to wheel her gently along to a room on the same floor without jolting the trolley in a lift or over uneven ground, and it was reassuring to be so close to the theatre if a patient had a post-operative crisis and had to return in a hurry. She shook off her soiled gown, and for the first time looked at the large round face of the clock on the theatre wall. Everything had happened so fast, there had been so many details needing her personal attention, and she had been so involved with the welfare of the patient in her charge that she had no idea of what was happening outside the small world of her ward and the operating theatre.

For her, no person had existed but the shrouded green-clad figures and the helpless woman on the table. She had watched while Slade Forsythe carefully found a way through the mass of free blood that filled the distended abdomen, helping him and anticipating his needs; she had checked the used swabs and instruments and fixed the final dressing, and now it was eleven o'clock at night.

Eleven? Surely that was impossible. Anna stared at the clock, her face pale. She had promised to meet Rob at nine, after she came off duty. She sank on to the anaesthetist's chair, and was suddenly faint. Rob . . . he would have waited and waited, and then taken it for granted that she had no intention of marrying him.

And did she want to do so? She was appalled at her unforgivable lapse, but it was an indisputable fact that she had forgotten Rob for three hours while the emergency needed her attention. I suppose I could go

125

down and see if he is there, she thought, but Claud would have left the lodge hours ago and it would be of no use ringing the main lodge to see if Dr. Delaney was there.

He'll have heard of the ectopic . . . all the hospital will have heard by now, she thought. It's such a rare case that they will have talked about it at supper and in the common rooms. He *must* have heard. She rang the main lodge to see if a message had been left for her but there was nothing.

Anna began to panic. She must find Rob and tell him . . . but what would she tell him? She looked round the silent theatre and knew that she could not leave Beattie's yet, not before she had worked here for a while, become a part of its history. She loved the old place, and now she loved the new block. It wasn't buildings that made a tradition, it was people and the quality of the work they did.

A lone figure stood in the doorway, the light behind him. He was tall and young, and was only in silhouette. Anna started.

"Rob?" The man hesitated and took a step into the room. "I'm sorry," she said.

"Not Delaney, I'm afraid. I hope I didn't keep you too late." Slade Forsythe looked very tired. "I want to thank you," he said, as if the words were being forced from him.

"There's no need, I was only doing the work I came here to do," replied Anna. The gulf between then had never been wider, the coldness of the Slade Forsythe Ice Age had returned, and she was sad. He had seen Rob kissing her last night and must have drawn his own conclusions. What did it matter if he disliked Rob? It

126

was not his concern, and he had no right to let it affect his attitude towards her. Her private life was her own, wasn't it?

But she couldn't be really annoyed. He was tired and serious, having not shaken off the drama and tension of the past few hours.

"Some Sisters assist adequately; you are all a surgeon could wish for, Sister." A glimmer of humour softened the lines of his mouth. "I hope that if I am ever under the knife, you will be there to make sure nothing is overlooked."

"I return the compliment," said Anna with dignity. "It was a pleasure to watch you and to be involved."

"We make a good team . . . Sister," he said, and turned quickly and was gone. Anna felt that he had begun to say something different . . . even to call her Anna again, but the moment had gone. She changed and adjusted the lace bow beneath her chin and was ready to leave. The night staff were busy and the patient in the side ward had recovered from the anaesthetic, been made comfortable although she still lay flat with one pillow, and was now asleep. There was no need to linger, but Anna found it difficult to face the night, the road by the lodge and the nurses' home.

Slade Forsythe would be there in his room; and Rob? Would he be waiting where she found him last night? She knew that she could not go away with him, and it filled her with sadness. She loved him still, but it was not the kind of love that she wanted. With Rob, she would never have anything deeper than a wonderful sex life and she knew that sooner or later, he would revert to being a womaniser, however much he vowed to the contrary.

Two years ago she would have married him and ignored the warning signals, but did she really want to go through the next few years, trailing after him with no career of her own, and devoting herself to building up his ego?

She pushed open the outer door and breathed deeply. The night was full of stars and the air was mild. She let her cloak swing free and walked towards the nurses' home.

The light in her corridor was on and the carved wooden chairs were empty. Anna didn't know if she was glad or sorry to find nobody there, but listlessly unlocked her door. Her long green cloak flowed over the chair, showing the scarlet lining. She took off her cap and ran her fingers through her hair.

"I'm tired and I'm in no state to decide anything, let alone what I want to do with my future," she thought. She was thirsty after she had bathed and changed into her nightdress and kimono and wondered if it would help her to unwind if she made a hot drink. It was after midnight, and she was sure that the small kitchen and sitting-room would be deserted. She had eaten no supper except for a sandwich she had eaten in her office and she was very hungry.

She stole down the stairs, taking with her some cheese that she kept for emergencies, knowing that there was bread and butter in the larder. She heated water and milk and closed the door. The thought of toasted cheese was irresistible; if she made sure the door was closed tightly, no one would smell the cheese. The new tin of ground coffee that she had bought only last week sent up a fragrant aroma, and her mouth watered. She put two large slices of bread under the

128

grill and grated the cheese. When one side of the bread was golden brown, she turned it and spread the cheese evenly over the slices, turning the gas high as she returned the pan under the grill.

A satisfying sizzle told her that the cheese was ready, bubbling hot and tinged with brown. She carried the tray into the sitting-room and turned on the electric heater.

Anna sipped the coffee and wondered why it always tasted better late at night, when it was supposed to be bad for her and would probably keep her awake. She dug her teeth into the first luscious slice and heard the door open.

For a moment she thought it must be Susan, who had theatre tickets and would have come in late, although even Susan must be in by now. Guiltily, she suspected that the smell of toast had filtered upwards to one of the bedrooms and that someone had come to check that the house wasn't on fire! She craned her head round the side of the wing chair in which she was curled up, and to her horror, saw that it wasn't Susan, or any of the nursing staff who stood there in the doorway; it was Slade Forsythe.

"Hello," Anna greeted him weakly. "Do you like toasted cheese?"

The expression on his face was a comical mixture of surprise, embarrassment and reluctant admiration. Anna sank more deeply into the chair, acutely conscious that she was wearing only a thin nightdress and the silk kimono that her uncle had brought home from Hong Kong. The dark green velvet of the chair's upholstery made the colours of the kimono even brighter, and as she put up a hand to smooth the dark hair away from her eyes, a gleam of gold embroidery glowed with a rich light.

"I'm sorry," he said, "I . . . had to do a late round and I . . ."

Seeing his discomfiture gave Anna back her poise. After all, he saw women in dressing-gowns and much less every day of his working life, so it couldn't be a strange situation. She was well concealed beneath the voluminous robe, and she had as much right as he had to be in the sitting-room at this late hour. "And you smelled toasted cheese and wondered who was cooking at . . . good grief, nearly one o'clock in the morning!"

He grinned. "Something like that. I thought that only insomniacs, night nurses or over-worked doctors would bother with food at this hour." He was embarrassed again.

"And you thought that whoever it was, they would take pity on you and share their supper with you." Anna stood up and smiled. It was so silly to act as if they were complete strangers, however much they tried to avoid each other. They were neighbours and colleagues, and it was never possible to work with a man in such intensely dramatic circumstances and then to revert completely to the nodding acquaintance of people who happened to work in the same building.

We've got over one hurdle, she thought. Now it should be easier to talk, as we have our work in common and personalities need have no part in our conversation.

"I'll make some more coffee while you put what bread you can eat under the grill," she offered.

"But you need your sleep. I can make a cup of instant coffee, but I'd be grateful for some cheese if you can spare it." The atmosphere had eased into a warmer if still impersonal feeling and Anna was relieved. "Had you been to sleep?" he asked, glancing at her kimono.

"No, I had a bath and read and then the pangs of hunger caught up with me." She laughed. "So you caught me with my secret vice . . . toasted cheese."

She took a bite of toast and handed him the second slice. He protested but she waved it away. "Don't worry. I'm not going without! We can eat this first and have two fresh slices after the coffee has brewed." She poured the last half-a-cup of her own coffee from the brown pot. He tasted it and nodded approval. Anna sliced more cheese and put it on the fresh toast.

"Not only is she the most efficient Sister in Beattie's, she can make coffee, too," said Slade with mock reverence.

Anna blushed. "There's no end to my talents," she agreed.

"I guessed as much," he said, and something in the low voice caused Anna's heart to miss a beat. She turned away to make the coffee. "Can I help?" he asked, but Anna knew that at that moment she dared have no physical contact with the man who watched her with such brooding, enigmatic eyes.

Does he like me, she wondered, or does he dislike me so much that he has to pay me tiny awkward compliments to prove that he can be human? What does he think of women now that Carmel has gone?

She remembered that he had taken Carmel out because, according to him and, surprisingly, Rob had said as much, too, he had been in love with another girl and had used Carmel to hide the fact. Who was the girl

131

who he had taken such care should not be known to have anything to do with him? She watched him peering under the grill and grimacing as his fingers touched the hot toast. He searched in the cupboard and emerged triumphant.

"Worcester Sauce!" he said, and proceeded to sprinkle some on his cheese. "Want some?" Anna laughed, and he urged, "It makes all the difference. It takes this magnificent dish out of the merely wonderful into the sublime gourmet class!"

Anna held out her plate. "This is obviously the time when all our secret vices are revealed." She could have bitten off the words, but it was too late. She blushed deeply as he glanced at her, but he chose to ignore what she had said and carried the tray into the sitting-room. "We could eat it here," said Anna. "It's very late."

"Even past the witching hour," he said. "Sit down in that green chair again . . . it suits you, Anna." He handed her a mug of coffee and a plate. "This is very good. I haven't eaten this since I stayed with a rather odd aunt when I was a boy. She gave me toasted cheese and fizzy lemonade and I was sick."

Anna curled up in the chair and listened, her hands round the hot mug, absorbing the warmth, enjoying the food and most of all, wondering at the sudden boyish appeal of the usually sombre face.

"I hope you don't make a habit of being sick after eating such things," she said. "I'll remember never to give you fizzy pop with toasted cheese." Oh, dear, she thought, I've done it again. As if we shall ever find ourselves in this situation again! After tonight, I shall call him Mr. Forsythe and he will call me Sister. But I've never called him anything but Mr. Forsythe. Even

132

at the dinner, I funked it and called him 'you' or nothing at all.

He took the last slice after offering it to her. It was good to see him tucking in with all the pleasure of a boy eating his first chocolate sundae, or some other exotic food that tastes so good when one is really hungry. "Toasted cheese and coffee . . . real coffee, with guess what to follow?" She shook her head. "Grateful patient gave me these." He went into the kitchen and came back with two small knives and handed her a large, ripe peach.

"They must have cost the earth," he said. "But don't let that worry you. Plenty more where these came from, I beieve. The car tycoon in the private wing sent his wife to see Sir Horace last week, and she was enchanted by the old boy. Brought these in for the firm."

"Is she likely to come in to us? Just for a few days, under observation? Just for a rest? Just to bring in some more . . . ouch!" The peach juice ran down her chin and Slade Forsythe leaned forward and wiped her kimono with a large white tissue. She took it from him. His action was instinctive, protective, and gentle with no sexual undertones, but it was like an ache of exquisite, remembered pain to have him touch her, quite different from the surging lift of growing desire that she had felt whenever Rob touched her. "Thank you," she said softly.

"She only needed some hormone treatment which Sir Horace assured her would lift her depression and cut out her other menopausal symptoms. She was delighted."

Anna sucked the peach-stone and put it on the plate. Slade smiled, and thought how small and fragile she looked, curled up in the huge chair with the swirls of colour and gold swathing her so that only her piquant face, framed with dair hair, and one small foot peeping out from under the robe were visible.

She yawned. "Even coffee isn't going to keep me awake tonight," she said. She unwound herself from the chair cushions and picked up the remnants of the feast. At the sink Slade handed her the tea-towel. "There's no need for you –" she began as he splashed water into the sink.

"You wipe," he said firmly. "You'll get those lovely sleeves wet if you mess about with washing up."

At least he noticed that much, she thought. They gathered up the rest of the cheese, the remaining peaches and the coffee and crept upstairs. A distant clock struck the hour and a sense of unreality filled the silent corridor as if they were dream-walking. Anna nearly dropped the coffee as she groped for her key and Slade took it from her while she unlocked her door. He put the packages on the small table inside the door and stood back, regarding her with eyes that held something in their depths that almost frightened her. She lowered her eyelids and he put two more peaches into her hands. She laid them carefully on the table.

"Thank you," she said softly. "They are beautiful."

"Beautiful . . . the skin of a peach," he said and she looked up, startled to find him looking at her. They seemed to come together in spite of themselves as if some other force gently thrust them into each other's arms. His chest was hard against her softness, his lips warm and soft on her mouth, and she felt as if she could melt into his body, his heart and into his life, but she knew that this was the man who loved an unknown girl

. . . a man who was as lonely and as lost as she was. She loved Rob, didn't she? Only Rob could make her feel as if all the bells of heaven were ringing. And he had a secret love who did the same for him.

She broke away and fled into the safety of her room, hearing his voice, feeling the hands that let her go with such reluctance.

"Damn!" she heard. "Damn that man. Oh, what the hell! Forgive me, Anna."

She sank on to the bed and burst into tears. If she loved Rob, then why did she have this terrible emptiness in her heart? If she loved Rob, why did the memory of those dark, haunted eyes remain with her in the dark, and why did her mind tell her as she drifted into sleep, *You love Slade Forsythe, you silly girl! You love him and he thinks you love Rob.*

CHAPTER SEVEN

"A TELEPHONE message for you, Sister."

Anna raised eyes that were still showing signs of a restless night. She had dreamed and the dreams had wakened her but she knew it was useless to try to think of nothing when all her being wanted Slade to come to her, saying he loved her. She had tried to tell herself that he would do so, but knew that the one kiss had been inevitable. What virile man would have been able to resist one kiss when a girl appeared before him dressed as she had been, in a silky kimono and nightdress?

Rob would have tried to take advantage of the opportunity, she knew. I wouldn't have escaped Rob last night, she thought, and wondered afresh where he was. The nurse repeated her message and Anna pulled her thoughts back to ward duties.

"Well, you took your time." A petulant voice came over the line and Anna saw, to her horror, that the call had been made over the hospital telephone.

"Rob?"

"Who else? Or did you think I was Slade Forsythe? I hear you had quite a time with him last night. That's the one reason I regret not doing surgery. One has such cosy, intimate little talks with the nursing staff in the surgeons' room after such satisfying work!"

"Stop it, Rob. I'm sorry about last night, but we can't talk about it over this phone," Anna said firmly.

"You're sorry! I waited and waited. Then I rang the ward, but not even a message."

"There wasn't time," she faltered, knowing that this was a lie. When the woman had come in, waxen-pale and desperately ill, she had thought of nothing but how she could help and what she must do to prepare the theatre so that nothing was left to chance. She had forgotten that Rob existed.

"There is always time to leave a message," he said, icily.

"I can't talk now," said Anna. "Sir Horace is coming to do his rounds in five minutes, and you know what he is for punctuality." She hesitated. "I really am sorry, Rob, but I expect you heard what the case was? I could do nothing about meeting you, and when I rang the main gate there was no message for me, so I went to bed."

"When are you off today?"

"This afternoon," she admitted reluctantly.

"I'll meet you at the gates to the park at two." He rang off, leaving her no time to say whether she would be there or not. So he wasn't in such a hurry to go, after all. Anna tidied her desk and dabbed a little makeup on the dark rings under her eyes, and when Sir Horace came in with his entourage of students, house surgeon and a girl from the X-ray department who arrived at the same time with a sheaf of envelopes, Anna was composed and ready, even though she lacked her usual sunny smile.

She glanced beyond the group of white-coated figures but Slade Forsythe was not there. She wondered if her heart beat quickly for relief or disappointment, but now she was in her official capacity as head of her ward and joint theatre sister of the small operating theatre, she had the assurance of someone who knows her job thoroughly.

Sir Horace nodded to her, and to the casual observer he seemed curt, but Anna saw the warmth in the deep-set eyes under their shaggy brows. He went on berating his unfortunate house surgeon for a trifling oversight, and the poor boy was reduced to a blushing jelly.

Anna made sure that the H.S. had the right notes as they approached each patient and she whispered details about the cases so that he could tell Sir Horace any late developments that had arisen during the night, and which he might not have had time to read up.

"What are you two whispering about?" demanded Sir Horace. The H.S. blushed again, but pointed out, fairly firmly, that the patient in the next bed had not even been officially admitted and he was getting all the details verbally, to save Sir Horace waiting until the notes had been written.

"Well, what are you waiting for, my boy?" said the great man. "Screen, Sister! We'll examine this lady now." He beamed at the apprehensive young woman in the corner bed. "You'd like that, wouldn't you, my dear? Lots of handsome young men, all coming to see how you are?" He smiled in a fatherly way and lowered his voice, bending over the bed. "We'll try not to embarrass you, my dear, and it helps us to have several opinions. Don't mind, do you?"

"No, Doctor." The patient looked relaxed and even flattered by all the attention, and Anna marvelled at the power of the man who could rule his staff with such firmness and yet instil in every individual patient the belief that she really mattered and in his hands, and would have the best treatment that was obtainable. This was true, for the reputation of Sir Horace was world-wide, his opinions treated with great respect and his operating techniques copied by many visiting surgeons.

He laid his hands gently on the woman's abdomen and pressed, watching her face as he did so. "Don't try to be brave," he said, "tell me if I hurt you." She winced slightly as he pressed more firmly into her right side, then he examined the other side and she didn't tense her muscles. He felt for her pulse and stood back, gesturing towards the patient and looking expectantly at the H.S.

"Go on, then, boy, she doesn't bite." Sir Horace turned away to consult some X-rays of another case and left the unhappy young man to examine the woman.

She let out a yelp as he touched the painful spot, and Sir Horace came back. "No need to do the operation with your bare hands, my boy! At least you found it. What is it? What do we do? How would you treat it?" He glanced round at the grinning faces of the students. "No, don't give these ignoramuses the benefit of your brains, Doctor . . . *you*!" He pointed to the boy who was still sniggering. "Discomfort of the right side. What questions do you ask?"

"How long she's had the pain?"

"She? And who is *she*? The lady has a name." Anna raised her eyebrows and exchanged glances that held pained amusement with the house surgeon. She hastily showed him the name at the top of the chart. It was a favourite trick of Sir Horace, to expect a student to know all the names in the ward where they were doing a round. He swung round to the house surgeon. "Her name, Doctor?"

"Mrs. Wendy Stanton," said the house surgeon, as if he had known her for years.

"Exactly," said Sir Horace, who until that moment had no idea who the lady was. "Remember," he said, sweeping the circle of faces with a frown. "In this hospital, the Princess Beatrice Hospital, we never refer to our patients as cases . . . except in notes and professional discussion. If I ever catch a student of mine calling a lady by her bed number or as 'the case of endometritis' . . . or whatever, I shall make him scrub for every emergency, night and day, for a month!"

The round proceeded, with Sir Horace in great form and his entourage following cautiously from bed to bed, taking hasty peeps at the charts and the patients' names as they went. It was all so familiar, the Olympian progress and the uneasy response of the students, the giggles of the patients when they had gone, but above all, the enhanced confidence of the women who felt that in Beattie's, they were safe and would be sent home better, if not cured.

Anna opened the door to the side ward very quietly. The nurse detailed to 'special' the case stood up and smiled. Sir Horace told the students to go on to the next ward and to examine two patients there. He glanced at the detailed chart and grunted his approval.

"Mrs. Ryan?" She opened her eyes. "You're doing very well, my dear." She smiled the smile of a woman who has sensed that death was very near and has come back through a deep, dark pit of pain and weakness. "You wanted that baby badly?"

Tears flowed from under the closed eyelids, and Anna wondered why Sir Horace had reminded the patient of what must be a tragedy. Why couldn't he have left all reference to the lost baby until she was stronger?

"We were so happy . . . we waited for years, and when I was pregnant, we were over the moon," she murmured.

"You still have one healthy ovary and tube. Come in when this has cleared and we'll see if we can't make sure that you can try again." She opened her eyes wide for the first time. "Now, concentrate on doing everything that Sister tells you and . . . don't give up hope. We might not be lucky, but with the help of a little treatment, we shall do our best."

Sir Horace turned to the house surgeon. "Make a note that Mrs. Ryan is to see me, personally, in three months' time."

Anna felt rather ashamed. Sir Horace might be brusque and often unfair where his students were concerned, but he knew that Mrs. Ryan must be worrying and grieving each time she woke from her drugged sleep. She curled up into a much more natural position in the bed and had her first normal sleep since the operation.

Anna saw that the drip had been removed. "When did Mr. Forsythe come in?" she said.

"He was here at six, Sister. He said he couldn't sleep and was a bit concerned about Mrs. Ryan, so he came and took the drip down and ordered her sedatives as she was very restless."

She handed the chart to Anna. The curve of the pulse rate had gone down and the temperature was still subnormal. Her blood pressure was rising to normal and her colour was better. Anna pointed out the dangers of a rising blood pressure after operation, as it was the time when strain would be put on any insecurely tied-off blood vessel and there could be a reactionary haemorrhage within the first twenty-four hours after an operation, but she was sure that she was only telling the nurse an academic point in the present circumstances. She recalled the care of the long slim fingers that tied and sutured, sealed with diathermy and swabbed again, to make sure that no bleeding points were left.

Slade had been here so early? Was it anxiety about his patients that had made sleep impossible? Or was it the fact that he felt guilty after taking her into his arms and kissing her?

This was no time for such conjectures, and Anna hurried back to her office to carry on with the work that had been left when Sir Horace made his round, and it was almost lunchtime before she could go back into the side ward to see Mrs. Ryan again.

She paused in the doorway while the nurse finished taking Mrs. Ryan's temperature. How pretty it was, she thought. The old building had only recently shed its dark brown and green paint and been jollied up with bright curtains and pastel-coloured emulsion, but it didn't really fit the heavy Victorian architecture. Tarted up was right, as if an old but dignified lady had dressed like a teenager, losing both elegance and dignity. The new block, designed for new equipment and modern décor, was more successful, and the clean lines of the wide windows with practical but well-chosen blinds and curtains helped the room to be a place of real rest and recovery. The bed was still tilted a little backwards, but Mrs. Ryan had two pillows now and looked very comfortable.

142

"Nearly up to normal, Sister," said the nurse. "Her blood pressure is stable and her respirations normal."

"Has Nurse told you to breathe deeply, Mrs. Ryan?" The woman nodded. "And have you done so?" Anna said with a smile.

"It hurts, Sister. I can't take a really deep breath. It hurts under my stitches and under my ribs."

"I know: that's difficult, but you must try. Take a deep breath now. Not a sudden intake, but gradually. It isn't great gasps of air that are needed, but you must fill your lungs to their capacity several times a day, or you may have trouble. You certainly won't get better as quickly as you'd like if you don't exercise your lungs."

The woman took a cautious breath and gasped. "It does hurt, Sister. Can't I leave it until tomorrow? I'm tired, and I feel so weak."

"Let me help you," said Anna. She peeled off her cuffs and rolled her sleeves high, slipping on the frilled bands to cover the rolled sleeves. She helped the nurse to lift Mrs. Ryan gently forward, and while the nurse held her, she put her own hands firmly round the woman's ribs.

"Now, gently, breathe in," said Anna taking the pressure. "Good . . . and again. Well done. Very good! Can you manage just one more?" Anna gently tapped the woman's back with the outer edges of her own hands, going systematically from waist to neck several times, then the breathing was done again.

Mrs. Ryan coughed and Anna placed a hand over the dressing and braced it to limit the pain, and they gently laid her back on to the freshly shaken pillows.

"Well done," said a deep voice. Anna turned to see Slade Forsythe standing there, leaning against the wall.

"Cough reflex back in working order, breathing exercises begun and general condition improving fast." His tone was light but he didn't smile. "You seem to have so many talents, Sister," he said, "I didn't know you were a physiotherapist as well as a ward sister, theatre sister and . . . cook." It was as if he had intended saying something different at the end but had thought better of it.

"And she's so gentle and kind, Doctor," put in Mrs. Ryan.

"Is she, now?" he said with a touch of cynicism. "It looked very much as if she was bullying you."

"Only in the nicest possible way, Doctor. I think she's wonderful, don't you? I . . . think you are all . . . wonderful," said Mrs. Ryan, sleepily.

"We are so busy being wonderful people," he answered, "some day, we may find that we are so wonderful that we have missed out ourselves." It was almost a whisper, and Anna was the only one to hear it. She drew the curtains slightly, to shut out the bright sunshine and gave the special nurse her orders.

Slade Forsythe still leaned against the wall, watching everything that went on in the room, his shoulders slightly hunched as if he were cold or very tired. Anna was confused. He was the most dedicated man she'd met. How then did he think he might lose by being immersed in his profession? Was the woman he loved nothing to do with medicine?

Could that be the reason, she wondered, why no one in the hospital had linked his name with anyone but Carmel? It would explain a great deal. If his love was not a doctor or a nurse, there was sure to be a pull of conflicting interests. To the layman, the life in such a busy hospital as Beattie's must seem a constant round of work and drudgery for little reward, with unsocial hours of work and very often, holidays and off duty times when friends outside the profession were at work, making it impossible to share free time.

Anna made up the chart and once more took the patient's pulse-rate. She glanced at Slade. "Have you any further orders, Mr. Forsythe?"

"No, she seems fine. We'll give her a rest until this evening and then go over her chest. You obviously don't need me to tell you the dangers of a chest complication after an operation of this nature. Anna nodded. "I was glad to see you doing a little gentle hacking. Did she cough up anything?"

"Yes. It may be clear now, but when I come on duty this evening, I'll do her again when you've finished examining her, if that's all right." She hesitated. "Unless you'd rather write her up for physio.?"

"No . . . we want to disturb her as little as possible, and you were doing fine." He looked at his watch. "Time to eat. Do you go now?" It was a polite question that he might ask of anyone.

"No," said Anna, "I'm off duty this afternoon, so I go to second lunch."

He nodded, gravely, and left, leaving Anna staring after him. You strange, cool creature, she thought. Not a hint about last night, no sign of any emotion or feeling for her other than was due to a very efficient colleague. I must have dreamed it . . . they say that after a case like that, one can't think straight.

She shrugged and sent her staff nurse to first lunch and made a quick round of the ward to make sure that each patient had the right lunch, especially the new admission who was a diabetic; a fact that she had not found necessary to tell the admissions clerk! Fortunately, a nurse who had worked on the diabetic wing had recognised her, and when her notes arrived, of course it was easy to check her history. But the wrong diet would have upset the patient and made it impossible for her small operation to be done the next day.

The staff nurse came back, thinking that the afternoon would go fairly quickly, and that with any luck she would be off duty promptly for an evening at the cinema to see a film she had missed twice because her off duty didn't coincide with performances.

Anna walked through the grounds before lunch, noticing the budding trees and the sudden shabbiness of the conifers and other evergreens that had made at least a patch of colour during the dull, cold days. It was like discarding an old love because a newer, brightly clothed one came on the scene. Am I being like that? she asked herself. Would I still be in love with Rob if I had never met Slade? But I'm not in love with either of them, she told herself firmly. A small voice came to her from her near-sleep the night before. *You are in love with Slade and he thinks that you love Rob.*

Would it make any difference if he thought that she had decided to say goodbye to Rob, to let him go away to the new job without her and to make a new life for herself at Beattie's? But the conviction that another woman held his heart filled her with a sadness that the coming of Spring could only make worse.

Spring was a time for love, for finding a mate. She smiled, glancing up at a bird that viewed her with shiny currant eyes.

"It must have been too cold even for you, this year,"

she said, remembering the snow on St. Valentine's day. The sun was warm on her face but she hurried into the dining-room. She had to meet Rob, even though she had not said she would. Oh, why must he come and upset me again? she thought. She had an uneasy feeling that Rob in the park, in Spring, might easily make her forget all her good resolutions concerning him.

I know he would never make a good husband, but do I want that? she thought. Am I ready to leave . . . all this, to settle down to raise a family and to run a home? But she knew that she would have to marry Rob or to tell him to go away for ever. For her there was no half-world of love, no furtive wearing of wedding rings in strange hotels and no casual sex. When I marry, she thought, it will be for ever . . . do the birds mate for ever? She had heard of swans mourning for their mates, but the tiny birds fluttering by the dining-room windows seemed much too frivolous.

Two other sisters had heard of the ruptured ectopic the night before. "I saw Mr. Forsythe this morning and put my big foot in my mouth," said Sister Smythe. "I said he'd had a good party, or something that meant he'd been on the town! He was quite rude. Then of course, I heard about the session in your theatre. Poor man! He looked as if he'd been up all night."

"He was . . . I believe," said Anna, and tried to change the subject. She could imagine Sister Smythe's eager eyes if she heard that Sister Anna Boswell and Mr. Forsythe had been eating toasted cheese at one o'clock in the nurses' home, with Anna clothed in very scanty and rather fetching night attire.

"I find that man rather hard to understand," she went on. "Sometimes he is charming, then he can be so

147

rude I want to slap him down. He has something on his mind. Anyone know anything? Has he a wife or lover tucked away somewhere? He's an absolute clam when I ask him anything about his home life." She sighed. "I gave up lusting after him long ago. I know when I'm beaten."

Anna helped herself to more vegetables. "I think he's completely dedicated to surgery," she said.

"Don't you believe it. A man like that couldn't be a medical monk. I used to drop everything I touched when he came into my ward, and even now I have my moments," Sister Smythe said, to the amusement of the others, who knew that she was devoted to her current boyfriend. "I think he's lovely, but he needs thawing out. We all know it's been a long, cold winter, but he hasn't realised that it's Spring, believe it or not! Anna, you ought to have a go at him! You're pretty and unattached. Come to think of it, you'd be very good for him."

Anna's cheeks flamed. She bent to pick up her table napkin to hide her confusion. Sister Smythe went on, "But I was forgetting. Claud told me about the flowers that came from a secret admirer, so you do have a hidden lover! Bad luck, Mr. Forsythe. What a pity, I thought I was such a good matchmaker." She pushed her plate away and left the table, saying that she wouldn't have pudding as she really must lose some weight before her holidays.

"You never told me you had a rich lover who sent you flowers?" said the other sister. "Oh . . . I remember. You had a boyfriend when you were training here. Didn't I see him the other day? So he sent you the flowers." She chuckled. "It's a wonder that Smythe hasn't sorted that out. She knows everything that goes on here. You have only to see her with Claud to know that someone's reputation is in the balance."

Anna thought about the flowers when she got to her room. She had never mentioned them to Rob and he had not said that he had sent them, but she couldn't think who else would send her expensive roses out of season. It was a memory that she liked to forget, feeling guilty and childish every time she recalled flinging perfectly beautiful flowers away. Did it matter that Rob had sent them? They were so lovely that they had a right to be enjoyed, even if her worst enemy had sent them, and Rob . . . he wasn't an enemy. He could never ben an enemy even though he had gone away with Carmel.

She dressed in a new pair of trousers that showed the slim line of her hips and topped it with a huge, floppy sweater of rich rust-red that made her look tiny under its extravagant folds. She matched up her lipstick with the colour of the wool and hoped that she looked sex-less.

She made a face in the mirror and ran a comb through her hair, releasing the long shining locks from the French pleat that she wore under her cap. The slight curve of the hair on her cheek made the creamy skin glow. She glanced at the last of the peaches on the dish and remembered what Slade had said, and how he looked when she admired the softness and colour of the peaches they had eaten in the sitting-room by the electric fire.

She turned away and picked up her shoulder bag. It was ten to two, and this time she knew she must be on time to meet Rob. She ran along the drive, past the

149

main gate and out of the little-used gate in the wall, away from the main block. The road was deserted except for a few badly parked cars left by students late for lectures or ward rounds. She smiled as she saw the beat-up old cars, several of them decorated with painted slogans or pictures of Snoopy or other cartoon characters. It was so obviously the work of students and she envied the uninhibited minds that liked to be thought different.

She thought of Slade Forsythe's car. It was sleek and high-powered, dark and efficient. Would it dare to break down when its lord and master drove it? It was like him, cool and efficient. But inside the car, she remembered, there had been comfort . . she had sunk back into the seat when he drove her, confident that she could trust Slade to drive her safely and to take care of her.

Anna shook herself. She was day-dreaming again. It was about time she realised that such men were not for her. He was in love with a girl, and for him there would be one woman and one alone to love . . . for ever. His single-minded attitude to his work would surely be the same in his private life.

She saw Rob's car parked by the wrought-iron gates leading to the grassy path through the park. Rob was like his car, too. The bonnet was long and powerful, the rear end cut down in a sweep that gave an exaggereated impression of speed, and the colour was flamboyant orange. A dent on one wing showed that someone had driven carelessly, and Anna suspected that it had been Rob Delaney.

Rob was leaning against the car and watching her approach. The sun shone down on to his fair hair, bringing out highlights of gold. 'Fair waves the golden corn,' thought Anna.

"Hello, Rob," was all she said. He smiled a trifle bleakly and her heart sank. This was going to be difficult, she thought. She remembered other occasions when she had annoyed him by keeping him waiting when she was late off duty. That had been two years ago, but his attitude was the same today. "I'm not late, am I?" she asked, and wondered why she had to sound guilty.

"No, for once you're on time . . . I'm flattered. I wondered if you'd bother to come at all."

Anna stopped and looked down at a loose stone that had fallen from the rockery bordering the path. "Rob," she said, quietly, "I am not late, I have come to meet you and if you can't be less sarcastic, I'm going away again. I couldn't help what happened last night. You, being a doctor, knew very well that I had no choice. I've explained, I tried to contact you after the case and I'm sorry. Now, for heaven's sake drop it."

He glanced at her flushed face with a wondering expression. Anna had changed. In the old days she would have taken all his criticism and listened humbly, anxious that he should not be angry and only too ready to think that any mistake in their arrangements for meeting must be her fault. This Anna had grown up. She was beautiful instead of just pretty, and she had developed independence and force of character. He saw the soft rise and fall of her breast under the ridiculous sweater, and he was filled with an aching desire that had its roots in remembered kisses and, if he was honest, in wounded pride.

When Carmel had gone to Ireland with him, he had

151

felt like a super-man. A beautiful tempestuous woman had flung herself at his feet and gone away with him. He had been her slave and her master, and the experience was shattering in its intensity. He recalled Carmel, totally abandoned in love and an almost insatiable desire for gifts and flattery. It had been wonderful while it lasted, but the fire that burns the brightest, with the highest flames, dies quickly, unless fed carefully with more stable fuel to produce a long-lasting glow. It had been so with them, and one day he had seen Carmel with another man and knew that it was finished.

He had been hurt and insulted to think that he had given so much of his time and life to her, but his feelings had held more than a tinge of relief and he longed for the fresh, flowerlike tenderness of Anna.

His pulse quickened. The new Anna could be everything he wanted. She was more desirable with this added spirit, and the swathes of thick hair that swung past her cheeks made him want to touch them, brush them aside and reveal the lovely line of her throat.

"I'm sorry, darling," he said. "I was so frightened last night, thinking that you had no intention of seeing me again, that I lost my temper." He shrugged. "You know me."

She looked up suddenly, and he was enchanted by the child-like clarity of her eyes, the whites blue-washed and the irises dark with emotion. "Yes, I do know you, Rob," she said quietly.

He sensed the prickly undertone to her words and laughed, tucking her hand under his arm and drawing her further into the park. "We have a lot to say, but let's just walk and enjoy the sun," he said. Anna was wary. "We can walk through the poplar grove, admire the blossom and go out of the far gate and have a drink or some coffee in the Falcon."

"They're shut," said Anna.

"Well, we'll go to a café . . . join the tea-urn set."

"All right, but I have to be back for duty this evening."

"Damn duty!" Once more his voice had a querulous edge. "I'm sorry, Anna . . . but we've hardly been together for five minutes, and you can't wait to get back."

"Rob, let's do as you said. Let's walk a little," placated Anna. In spite of her annoyance, she could not ignore his magnetism. Even the petulant curve of his mouth brought its aching memories, and she recalled his sweetness when everything between them was right. He squeezed her hand and entwined his fingers with hers, and she felt again the same thrill of physical contact that she had known . . . was it only two years ago?

They walked by the ornate sunken garden and the folly erected by the rich man who had endowed the park 'For the Recreation and Christian enjoyment of the Local People'. The plaque was still there, the copper green against the rough stone wall. Anna tried to hurry by, remembering too late that this was the place where they had first talked of love and marriage. He's brought me here deliberately, she thought.

"Remember the notice?" said Rob. "We never did establish what Christian enjoyment was, did we?"

This is the same conversation, continued, that we started here so long ago, she thought. She moved away from him, fumbling in her handbag for a tissue as an excuse to free her hand from his clasp. She turned back, as he was no longer by her side, and saw him beckoning

153

from the deep arched marble seat set in the far corner of the Italian garden. Her heart did strange things as she went slowly towards him.

"Come and sit down," Rob said easily. "You had a bad night and a busy morning. Take the weight of them." He sounded friendly, unconcerned, but Anna saw a glint in his eyes that showed that he was triumphant. He thinks he has me here where it all began, she thought. He thinks that he has only to recall old times and I shall fall into his arms again.

The magnolia tree was bursting into bloom. One of the buds lay on the path, torn from the bush by a hide-and-seek child. Anna picked it up and brushed the dust from the waxen petals. She inhaled the faint, sweet fragrance from the inside of the cupped petals and the scent reminded her of muted red roses.

Rob must love her, to have sent her roses like the ones she had received when she came to Beattie's. She stroked the cool flower and wondered why he had never told her that he had sent them.

Rob tried to take the flower from her, quite gently, but as if it was a barrier between them. "No, Rob. I want to keep it. It's so pretty. I've wanted a magnolia tree since I was tiny. My grandmother had one, and ..."

"Damn your grandmother!" he said, and seized her, crushing the flower between them in a wild embrace. His mouth was warm and full on her lips, his arms strong and merciless. He rained kisses on her face and again found her lips.

Anna struggled, feebly, aware of Rob as never before. She sensed his experience, his confident expertise and her fear left her. The moment she had dreaded had arrived. The decision regarding their future was made

154

as she lay passively in his arms, neither encouraging his kisses or repulsing them. The crushed fragrance of the flower seemed to seal the fate of their love, the past and the future.

He held her away from him, puzzled. "Damn it, Anna. I love you. I want to marry you . . . it isn't just . . ."

"It isn't like Carmel and you?"

"Is that what's wrong?" His confidence returned. "I do believe you're still jealous." He gave a condescending laugh. "Think no more of that little affair, darling. You know how it is . . . I can't imagine that you have been alone for two years, whatever you say!" He saw that she was smiling but in her smile was something that made him look anxious. "You *do* love me, Anna. You know you love me. I've come back to marry you." He brushed the crumpled petals from his jacket, hardly noticing what he did.

It would be like that with him, she realised. When he had finished with something, a place, a possession . . . a woman; it would be brushed away as if it had never existed. A great relief spread through her mind. At last I know the best and the worst, she thought. You *need* me, Rob. I would be the wife who sat at home and was expected to forget and to forgive when you came back to me from each new love affair. You need me and I think you love me, but I am cured, Doctor, I am free.

"I can't marry you, Rob," she said, simply.

"Who is he?" His voice was rough with pain and anger. He grasped her shoulders in a grip of steel and shook her. "Who is he?"

"Rob! You're hurting me. It's nobody. I'm not in love with anyone."

155

He swore, softly. "I might have known. I told you I didn't believe that you had been alone for two years. You're much too pretty. I suppose whoever it is has a cosy pad somewhere near the hospital?" For a moment, he faltered and looked uncertain. "But I thought you lived in the nurses' home."

He relaxed his grip and Anna slid away from him, standing by the magnolia tree. The scent of roses, she thought. She had to know . . . someone had sent her roses. If Rob had shown her that he loved her by sending expensive flowers, and convinced her that he respected her concern for her work and all living things . . . She stared at the lightly swaying blooms and picked one to take back to her room.

"Did you send me roses?" she said. It was his last chance to show an awareness of her sentiments.

"Did you send me roses?" she repeated as he looked blankly at her. He shook his head. "Someone sent me roses . . . lots of long-stemmed, crimson roses, out of season and very beautiful," she said, almost to herself.

"You know me . . . I never send flowers unless someone dies." He gave a short laugh. "I shouldn't worry about it. It's probably Sir Horace. He's the only one with that kind of money to throw away that you're likely to know." It was a familiar old ploy, to make her uneasy, to take away her confidence and to convince her that without Rob she would be nothing. Anna was grateful for every unpleasant facet of his character that emerged. It made it so much easier.

"Pick me a flower, now, Rob?" Her face was sweet, her voice pleading. He had renewed hope. He plucked a spray, tearing the bark badly and clumsily. He gave it to the woman he loved with all his being, to the woman he had been on the verge of losing. If that was all she wanted to keep her happy, he'd change his ideas and shower her with flowers.

She took it from him and kissed it lightly. "You're right, Rob. When there is a death, we should give flowers." She broke off one of the blooms and handed it back to him. "Something did die, Rob, dear. I'm sorry. I shall always love you in a special kind of way . . . but I could never marry you."

Her calm, sad voice did more to convince him of her sincerity than all the tears or ragings of a dying passion. He watched her departing back, slim and erect. Anna did not look back, but he saw the spray of flowers fall from her hand.

CHAPTER EIGHT

"SISTER . . . Sister Boswell!" Claud leaned out of the small window of the porter's lodge and waved. Anna started. She had walked by without seeing him and it was only when he shouted that she heard him call. "Got cloth ears or something? Shouted meself hoarse, I did," he grumbled.

"I'm sorry, Claud, I was miles away."

He regarded her with curiosity. She had walked down that path as if she was sleep-walking and Claud, being Claud, the porter who liked to know everything about everybody, was very intrigued. With the audacity of someone who was not directly under the discipline of the ruling medical and nursing bodies of the hospital and so led a life of certain privilege, he could afford to probe deeper. "Thought you had a date, Sister. Thought you were going out with Dr. Delaney."

She looked at him coldly. "So?"

"No offence, Sister," he said hastily. "I had a message for you, but I told them that you were out this afternoon. I thought you had a date," he added, as if that explained everything.

"Sometimes, I think you talk in riddles. Who rang or called?"

"The flower shop, Sister. They weren't clear what you wanted them to send to Lady Ritchie."

"Have you only just told them I wanted flowers sent? Really, Claud! I asked you to give the order because I knew I would have no time to see Michael myself. You forgot, didn't you?"

Anna was very annoyed. What must Lady Ritchie have thought? It was customary to send a thank-you note after being invited to dinner by Sir Horace and his wife, and the idea of sending flowers had seemed a good one at the time. Now, no letter or flowers had been sent.

"I sent the message, Sister, but they didn't have the pot-plant you wanted. He asked if freesias would do and I said yes unless he heard from you."

"And now someone hasn't sent them?"

"That's about it, Sister. Not my fault."

Anna sighed. "I'll walk down to the shop. I have time before I change back into uniform." It was a relief to have something definite to do to take away the memory of Rob's stricken face.

He really loves me, she thought. How ironic! Two years ago, I would have nearly died with pleasure at the thought of marrying him, and now I am empty of all feeling. Anna glanced in the window of the one dress shop and smiled at the thought of any of her patients blossoming in the weird smocks and trousers festooned against the bright hessian backcloth. The shop vainly hoped to cater for the young nurses, but had badly judged their taste. It would be the Sandras and Karens of the new wing who would buy these clothes eventually, when they were marked down at the sales.

The florist was talking on the telephone and Anna strolled round the shop, inhaling the sweet scent of spring flowers. She touched a damp fern and picked up a rather pretty vase, and wondered whether she could have a macramé hanging basket in her office.

"Sorry to keep you," said Michael. "He . . . your

porter, was very vague when he gave us the order, and I'm afraid we all got our lines crossed or something." He smiled. "But not to worry! You weren't the only one. One of the medics had the same trouble, and when we told him that your order had gone astray, he offered to take yours and deliver both lots to Lady R. He said it would save time and explanation and you could settle with us later." He called to a girl in the back room. "What did the doctor take to Lady R.? Sister Boswell's order?"

A girl came out of the back room and eyed Anna with interest. She was smiling in a faintly knowing manner. "It was freesias, Mr. Michael . . . not roses."

"I should hope not. Gratitude is one thing, extravagance another!" said Anna. "I could never afford roses at this time of the year."

"Well, he did."

Anna tried to think which of the doctors at the dinner party was likely to send Lady Ritchie roses. "It must have been Dr. Somerdale, the consultant," she said. The girl looked blank. "Short and fair with gold-rimmed glasses?"

"No." The girl giggled. "You have to be joking!" She picked up the telephone receiver and was immediately immersed in the intricacies of an enquiry about wedding bouquets.

Anna bought a bunch of violets and settled her bill for the freesias and strolled back, buying doughnuts and cream slices in the baker's as she went by, and couldn't resist the smell coming from the kitchens at the back. I can give some to Susan, she thought guiltily. I won't eat them all.

The walk was soothing and when she changed for

160

duty, she was once more calm and ready to face whatever might present itself that evening. She took the violets to her office and put them in a posy bowl by a dark green plant, the almost sombre purple glowing richly, and fortunately having no resemblance to the poignancy of the delicate magnolia blossom. After taking report from her staff nurse who was anxious to go off duty, Anna went into the side ward to see the patient who had been in the theatre the night before. Mrs. Ryan lay half-asleep, but she was smiling. Her colour was good, after being given several pints of transfused blood, and pain-killers to keep her feeling comfortable. She opened her eyes.

"Hello, Sister . . . the doctor came, but said he'd come back."

Anna glanced at the chart at the end of the bed, wondering if something was wrong. She asked which doctor had called, and gathered that first the house surgeon and then Mr. Forsythe had come.

"That's the one who said he'd come back. He wants to sound my chest and help you get my cough going again." Anna recalled that Slade Forsythe had said as much that morning, but she wondered why he hadn't left it to the house surgeon as Mrs. Ryan was so much better. The erratic course of the graph on the theatre monitor had no resemblance to the gentle curves on the ward chart after only twelve hours. Anna could hardly believe that the corpse-like figure on the operating table and this woman could be the same person.

"I think what did me a lot of good was the older doctor telling me not to give up hope, Sister. When I thought I would lose the baby, I wanted to die . . . it was selfish of me, as I have a good husband and a nice

161

home, but I could think of nothing but all the heartache we'd had trying to get a baby. Now I have another chance, and if necessary I'll go into a nursing home or any place Sir Horace suggests if a long rest will help. I know it might not work, but at least we can hope again." Her eyes filled with tears. "I didn't know quite how much it means to my husband. He was nearly in tears when I told him that we needn't yet give up hope completely." She reached out for a drink from the feeding-cup, but Anna took it away and poured lime juice into a tumbler, helping her to drink it through a flexible drinking straw. Mrs. Ryan sighed with pleasure. "I feel more civilised drinking like that. A drinking spout makes me think of very ill patients . . . accidents and hopeless cases."

"It's all very good for the morale. Sister Boswell is very good at supplying . . . the right refreshment at the right time." Anna gasped. "Sorry if I startled you, but I didn't want you to spill that stuff all over Mrs. Ryan."

"He's been standing there for ages, Sister."

"What a good thing we weren't discussing him," said Anna, trying to hide her confusion by laughing. "Can I get you anything, Mr. Forsythe?" Her tone was completely professional again. He regarded her gravely. "You wanted to examine Mrs. Ryan, I believe," she added.

He unhooked the stethoscope from his neck and came towards the bed. Anna folded the bedclothes back a little and Slade bent over the bed and gently placed the diaphragm of the instrument on the woman's skin. He listened with care and concentration, and nodded when he wanted to have the patient sitting forward. Anna had called a junior nurse to help her raise the

162

patient's shoulders from the bed, and Slade examined the back with his usual care. He smiled and put away the stethoscope, dropping it into the deep pocket of his white coat.

Anna looked up. "Did you want me to hack her at all?"

"You may go, Nurse. Sister and I will manage."

Anna raised her eyebrows. It wasn't like him to order her nurses to go when she had asked them to come and help, but she need have had no doubts as to his expertise. Gently, he took the full weight of the patient on his broad shoulder while Anna tapped away at the exposed back. He helped Mrs. Ryan to cough and to clear her lungs of any mucus, and Anna ached with tenderness as she watched the gentle strength of the man she knew she loved. He would be gentle with anyone in pain. With him, the woman he loved would never need to fear his occasional brusqueness. To a woman who loved him, that would be unimportant, a foil to his strength and kindness. The woman who married him would have a husband of integrity and constancy. It must be so, or his name would have been linked with one or more of the nursing staff before now.

Anna could hardly continue. She smelled the scent of fresh linen and masculine after-shave, her fingers touched his as they helped Mrs. Ryan into another position and the touch left Anna in an agony of longing. She glanced at the stern profile. Had those lips kissed her . . . just once?

"That's enough. You have just the right touch, Sister." Anna was glad that her blush could be put down to physical effort. She was slightly breathless. He looked solemn.

"Shall I ring for Nurse now? I think I'll make the bed and settle Mrs. Ryan. You feel like a nap?" she said, and turned to ring the bell.

"Don't bother. I expect they're busy with suppers." Slade grinned, and his face had a boyish quality. "Will you trust me to make hospital corners, Sister? I assure you, I had plenty of practise when I did my midwifery."

He proceeded to fold blankets, and mitred the corners of the bedclothes with a flourish. Anna was amused and touched. Had he sensed her unease, remembering that kiss? Had he made a conscious effort to reassure her and to convey to her that what happened in the corridor outisde her room was light-hearted nonsense? She blessed his tact but a corner of her mind cried: *It wasn't just a kiss . . . I love you*.

At last all was neat, the curtains were closed against the evening light and the night shade fixed over the small observation lamp. Mrs. Ryan sighed. Slade loomed large in the dusk of the room. He picked up the notes from the bed end.

"May I borrow your office, Sister? I want to write up these notes and I have some X-rays to check. The viewer in your room is one of the best in the hospital." He held out a hand for his watch which he had left on the bed-table, and as he took it, he seemed to catch at Anna's hand for a moment. They stood as if frozen, and Anna wondered if he too had sensed the thread of gold that formed, slender as a cobweb and as fragile, connecting them for a brief morsel of time. Then he had gone, and Anna turned to push a drink near to Mrs. Ryan's hand.

I shall have to leave Beattie's, Anna thought as she smiled mechanically at the patients as she made her night round. I shall have to go. It would be impossible for me to work with him feeling as I do. I must look for another job somewhere far away.

It was unfair that she had braced herself to face Beattie's, knowing that its associations with Rob would colour eveything there, and now Rob wasn't important any more. She could work here quite happily knowing that she didn't love Rob, but Slade wouldn't go away; he was a part of Beattie's, just as she had imagined herself to be a part of the hospital. She must go.

The light in her office was dimmed and the door was shut. He seemed to be taking a long time to examine the X-rays. Through the frosted glass door she saw his tall figure standing by the viewer, and then the light went on and Slade sat at her desk, his head bent over the notes. When she returned from the dining-room he was still there, although the doctors had meals at roughly the same time as the sisters. Second sitting went by and he was still busy. Anna peeped in, but he was absorbed in work he had not done the previous day as he had been occupied by emergencies. How tired he looks, thought Anna and asked the junior nurse to put a cup of coffee on the desk for him. He accepted it gratefully and swore softly when he noticed the time.

"Thanks, Nurse. I can use that. I'll never get finished if I don't get on. I shall have to grab a snack later," he said when she asked shyly if he had missed dinner.

The night staff came on duty and Anna gave report, telling them to leave Mrs. Ryan to sleep as long as possible but to keep a close watch on her at frequent intervals. The time for a reactionary bleed had passed, but there were other complications for which they must watch carefully. At the door of her office, Anna hesitated. Her bag and notes were there, but she didn't want to disturb Slade Forsythe when he was so busy. She opened the door, softly, and saw him hunched over the papers, a look of deep sorrow on his face. She wondered which of his patients was so ill that he cared that much about her . . . or was it a secret sorrow that she had surprised?

He turned. "I hope I didn't disturb you," Anna said. "It's getting late, you know. You've had nothing to eat and you must be starving. If you go down to the kitchens now, they'll still have something edible."

"No. I'll go up to the Falcon later, if we have a quiet night." His smile was forced. "You have a date, I expect. Have fun."

"Let me make you some more coffee," offered Anna.

"You'll be late . . . and I don't think he likes to be kept waiting. He made enough fuss about last night because you worked late."

"I have no date," said Anna, drooping her long eyelashes and not daring to look at him. "I'll make you some coffee."

"No," he spoke sharply. "I'm grateful," he added, "but I have two patients to see who are due for surgery in the morning. I have several loose ends to tie before I can relax." He stared at her as she gathered her cloak and bag from the chair. He glanced at the violets in the shallow bowl. "I thought you didn't like flowers . . . even when they are a gift . . . a thank-you and a peace offering." His voice was bitter. "Flowers to say welcome."

"I love flowers," she said.

166

"But only if they are given by the right people?" He picked up his notes and brushed past her and out of the room. One folder fell to the floor and Anna picked it up, meaning to return it to records, but when she reached her room it was still in her hand.

A gift of flowers . . . a thank-you and a peace offering . . . or a welcome? She was cold with a mixture of fear and hopelessness. Had he sent them? No! It was impossible.

But Rob had not sent her roses, Sir Horace had sent none and the description she had given the girl in Michael's shop had only reduced the girl to giggles. Anna sank on to the bed. If Slade had sent them, what did it mean? She saw again the beautiful roses thrust into her waste-bin, discarded as unwanted rubbish when she thought that it was Rob who had sent them. She recalled seeing Slade as she went to empty the bin and she wondered if that had been a single rose in his hand as the door closed. Oh, *no*!

What must he think of her? He had made a gesture of friendship and she had spurned it in the worst possible way. Red roses were for friendship? Slade Forsythe must have thought so, while she had taken them to mean a sign of Rob's desire . . . red roses for love!

Scurrying figures passed her as she went to the nurses' home as student nurses escaped to change for the weekly disco in the medical school. Anna stood aside to let three breathless girls in before her and heard them clatter up the back stairs to their rooms. They were so lighthearted, so eager to see what talent the medical school could produce, secure in the knowledge that they would be very welcome as the teaching hospital was large and included a dental school, making a

167

good response from the nurses essential if the evening was to be a success.

Anna thought back to similar evenings when she had danced with Rob. She had been naive and breathless then, and it had been good. She shook herself and let herself into her room. Sitting on her bed, she let her thoughts wander again, to Rob and Carmel. Slade Forsythe had been seen with Carmel, but she now knew that he had only dated her to hide his real passion for an unknown girl. Had he sent flowers to Carmel? Had he sent the roses that Anna thought came from Rob?

She passed a hand over her weary eyes. I shall never know, she thought, and reached for the latest copy of the *Nursing Mirror* to see if another theatre job was advertised.

Laughter and running feet told her that the young nurses were using the forbidden front staircase as a short cut to the door nearest the medical school. Anna sniled in spite of her preoccupation, as she recalled seeing Slade Forsythe and Carmel at one of the disco evenings.

She was suddenly alert. It was that evening when Carmel had made a play for Rob, dancing before him sinuously, her tight sweater showing the raised nipples under the thin silk. She had swayed and danced with all the supple grace of someone with passionate Latin blood in her veins, and Anna had been very jealous of the glint that came to Rob's eyes as he watched, fascinated. Slade Forsythe had tried to persuade Carmel to go for a drink to the nondescript little pub that had been in the same position as the one the new Falcon now filled so well. Carmel had refused, saying that she wanted something more exciting, and when Rob pleaded pressure of work, notes he had to write before the next morning, Anna had gone miserably to her room wondering if they were together.

At that dance, a now dim figure had danced with her, not saying much but giving Anna strength, in a curious way, by just being there. At the time, she had been so full of her own misery that she had taken no notice of him.

Slade! she thought. You stayed with me when they went outside for a while . . . you tried to make Carmel go with you, knowing that Rob was hurting me . . . you were there, and I never even thanked you for your kindness.

It was a very real kindness, she thought. Because he had been suffering over his own secret love, Slade must have understood how she felt and hated seeing another human being enduring what he had endured. His compassion had made him take her under his wing and to try and restore the bond between her and Rob.

The thought only added to her unhappiness. She knew that she loved Slade with a deeper, richer emotion than she had ever felt for Rob, and now she was finding the deep truths of his wonderful character. That stern face, that total commitment to his work, had made him seem cold and forbidding; but the glimpse of the real heart of the man made her sick with yearning. Not with a feverish desire for physical love, although that was there, too, but for a deep sense of belonging that she knew she could find in his arms, if only he loved her.

I can only hope that I can be as generous as he when I discover who it is he loves; I can't guarantee to like her, she admitted to herself. But she silently vowed that if she could help him to happiness, even if it meant her going away and never seeing him again, then she would do her best.

The calm of resignation enfolded her as if she had taken religious vows and relinquished the world. Anna turned over the pages of the magazine again and made pencil marks by three advertisements. At least I should have good references from Sir Horace, she thought.

A tap on the door brought her back to reality. "Yes?" she called. "Come in."

Instead of Susan, who had mentioned the disco and wanted Anna to go to it, threatening to come and drag her out of bed to go there if necessary, it was Slade who stood there, still wearing his white coat.

"Hello," Anna said feebly, "you're off late."

His glance fell on the folder that Anna had brought over to her room by mistake. "Is that Mrs. Anderson's notes?" His voice held no rebuke, only a dull tiredness.

"I'm sorry," Anna apologised. "You dropped them, and I was going to push them under your door as medical records was shut." He stepped forward to take them. "Is it urgent? You look as if you've done enough for one day," she said.

"No, I'd finished with them but I wondered where I'd left them, as Sir Horace will need them at the clinic tomorrow." He yawned. "I'm glad I stayed on. I've caught up with all the notes, and I'm feeling very self-righteous." A smile lit his tired face.

"I'm glad . . . I know the feeling. Sometimes everything piles up, and it's never stuff that you can pass on to juniors. It's such a relief to get everything under control."

"That's how you like to run your department . . . I noticed." She blushed. "Is that how you run your life, too, Anna?" There was an edge to his voice. "Have you finally got Delaney organised? I suppose you made a few plans today."

His eyes told her that he had seen the pencil marks on the advertisements. "You don't waste time. Have you found a job near to his?" He picked up the magazine, looking puzzled. "I thought he had a job in Canada?"

He read the paragraph about the new clinic in Scotland, the post in a lush Bournemouth nursing home and the application form for V.S.O. None of them for work in Canada. He looked up and their eyes met. The sorrow he saw in her eyes convinced him that once more she loved Rob, and he was leaving her. The sorrow that she saw convinced her that for some reason he was desperately unhappy and she would never be able to help him.

"Oh! There you are. Really, Anna, even you must be well and truly off duty by now. Still in uniform? Oh . . . sorry, did something crop up after I went?" Susan took in the sight of Slade Forsythe still in his white coat, holding notes of a patient on the gynae. wing. "Not a panic tonight, surely? Do you need me?"

Slade glanced at the high-heeled, slender strip sandals and softly draped skirt that Susan was wearing. Her makeup was perfect and her hair shone. A fine gold chain hung in her cleavage where the bright blouse parted. He grinned.

"What would you say if I asked you to scrub up for a Caesar?" They all laughed. "Tonight," he told them, "I have told the opposition that I have gone to the dance. I am not to be disturbed and they must cope without our unit. Besides which, we have no empty beds. That leaves us fairly safe for one night."

"I didn't know you danced," Susan smiled. "What are you both waiting for? Go and get rid of that terrible coat, and I'll help Anna to change."

"I'm not going . . . I told you," said Anna. "And I don't think that Mr. Forsythe intended going either. He's been working all the evening and I don't think he's had anything to eat."

"What I'd really like," said Slade, "is some toasted cheese." His smile was enigmatic but Anna felt her colour rising.

"Funny," said Susan, "I thought I smelled cheese cooking the other evening . . . in the middle of the night, to be more exact. Was that you?" He grinned. "Shall I make some while you change? Or wait until you come to the disco? There's masses to eat there."

"What a good idea. I think you need a break too," he said, looking at Anna.

He thinks he's being kind again, she thought. He's seen the ads. and knows now that I'm not going with Rob. Poor man, he thinks that Rob has left me again.

She demurred, but Susan would take no refusal. She hustled Slade out to his own room and opened Anna's wardrobe, ignoring her protests. She selected a new dress of finely pleated silk, graceful and almost Victorian, with flowing sleeves and masses of tiny buttons on the tight bodice. Peacock colours of green and blue blended like the swift passing of a dragonfly, and an antique locket completed the picture.

Slade Forsythe was ready, dressed with casual elegance, and Anna knew that every head would turn to look at him as he went into a bar or a room full of people. He seemed to have shed his tiredness, and Anna began to enjoy herself.

172

Why not make the most of the present? she thought. She would leave soon enough. He believed that Rob had left her and could never know that her feelings were quite differently set. He would never know that she loved him. It would be torture and bliss to dance with him and she was safe.

The noise was fairly loud and conversation limited. Slade excused himself, pleading instant starvation if he didn't consume at least six sausage rolls at once. Anna saw his dark head above the crowd for an instant, and was swept away to dance the latest frenetic dance that was sweeping the discothéques of Europe.

She loved dancing, and soon the sheer pleasure of movement soothed away her weariness and brought a glow to her face. There was so much left to her even if she could never marry the man she loved. Men found her attractive; that was obvious from the way she changed partners so frequently, having no time to rest between dances. The hall was packed with young people all trying to talk above the music and Anna gave up trying to talk but smiled and danced and smiled.

The group left the stand for a break and someone sat at the piano and doodled a few melodies. He was one of the older registrars who arranged the dances, having taken an active part, playing a drum kit, in his student days. He ran through a few more numbers, softly, until someone dragged a mike near to the piano.

"Play something smoochy . . . douse the lights," called a voice. A burst of laughter greeted this, and someone dimmed the lights while a single spot hovered over the piano. He began at first in an exaggerated, theatrical way, as if sending up the golden-oldie scene, but gradually the tuneful melodies took over and the floor became filled with couples moving slowly, held closely and becoming sentimental.

Anna felt a touch on her arm and looked up at the dark shadow poised before her. She rose, with a wildly beating heart and slipped into the arms of the man who had kissed her just once outside her bedroom door. He said nothing, and they moved in unison, complete with the music and with the mood of the song heavy around them.

The man at the piano was singing in a pleasant low voice and as they passed by the words came clearly . . . "You will find your true love . . . across a crowded room . . . once you have found her, never let her go, once you have found her . . . never let her go."

The sharpness of tears pricked at Anna's eyelids as she was taken along on the tide of sound, her feet barely touching the ground. Slade was holding her close, his face against her hair, but other couples were doing the same . . . it was all a part of the mood, the dance and the night.

She closed her eyes and relaxed against him, savouring his nearness, storing up the moment to treasure when she was far away. The music stopped, but he held her as if unwilling to break the spell then the lights blazed, everyone began to laugh again and the group adjusted the mike to blare out hard Rock.

Anna excused herself to go to the powder room and recovered her poise. Susan sank down beside Slade and began to tell him about some of the people dancing. She was very amusing, and she wondered why he just watched her as if he heard nothing, a bitter smile etched on his face.

"What was that?" he said, suddenly all attention.

"What was what? I've been rabbiting on for ten minutes and you haven't heard a word . . . which bit was it?" Susan asked cheerfully. "I wish my fiancé was here. I may seem carefree . . . and from the groping I've had tonight, you'd think I was fancy-free, too, but I do miss him something chronic!"

"You were talking about . . . Anna."

"Oh . . . what was I saying?" Something in his voice made her look at him more closely. His face was pale, his eyes glittered with a strange light as if flecks of gold had appeared from behind the dark glow. But that was absurd. All eyes, blue, grey or brown looked dark in this grotty lighting, she thought. There was an urgency in his voice as he asked again.

"I was saying that now Anna has finally decided to get shot of that creep she's been in love with for so long, she might blossom out a bit and find someone she can really love." She sipped her orange squash and made a face. "You can taste the saccharine in this."

"Delaney? Where is he?"

"Hasn't she told you? I should have thought you had time to exchange your complete life stories during that last dance . . . very cosy and ear-nibbling, those dances," said the outrageous girl. "She told him that she doesn't love him and she has no intention of going to Canada or any other place with him." She regarded Slade coolly, a sudden idea striking her. "I think she's in love with someone . . . really in love." His mouth tightened and she knew that it mattered to him.

"Then why answer advertisements for jobs away from Beattie's? I saw her with the *Mirror* and I think she really means to leave."

"Wasn't it President Truman who said, "If you can't
175

stand the heat, get out of the kitchen'? I wonder . . ."
Susan mused cryptically, then picked up her empty
glass and as Anna returned, swept past her to the
refreshment bar.

Anna glanced as Susan's back and then at Slade. He
looked bemused. Anna smiled. "Has Susan been blind-
ing you with the science of the fine points of Rock?"

"No, just opening my eyes," he said softly. "You look
warm. I'm very warm, and I'd like a cold beer, not this
lukewarm cloudy stuff they have in that barrel. Come!"

It was said gently, but it was an order she had no
power to refuse. They slipped away to his car and in a
little while the river lights glowed and they arrived on
the embankment where a huge boat was moored on the
Thames. Coloured lights and soft rays of opalescence
outlined the ship, and from its depths soft music came
in a flood of sensuous invitation. They walked on and
came to another boat, similar to the first but smaller.
Anna asked if they were floating hotels, and Slade
explained that the first was a whole complex of entertainment which included restaurants, discos and bars,
but the second was quieter, more exclusive and much
more luxurious.

"Have you been there?" said Anna.

Slade searched in his wallet and found a card. "Sir
Horace has some very weird connections," he said.
"This is an exclusive club, and I have cards for five
clubs and one casino since I started working on his
firm. I came here last week . . . to see if it was suitable."

"Suitable for what? Does one eat there?"

He put a hand under her elbow and guided her to the
wide, carpet covered gang-plank. "We'll have some
wine and watch the river. Frankly, I thought it would

be very artificial and just another commercial proposition, but I think it has a certain charm."

A girl dressed in a very abbreviated version of a sailor's uniform greeted them and glanced at the card. A large man in well-cut evening dress beckoned, and they followed him through the dimly-lit passageway to a huge, low-ceilinged room with windows the whole length of one side. Tiny lights shone through a dark canvas like bright stars in a cloudless sky, and the banquettes facing the windows were high-backed and velvet-covered.

"It's lovely," said Anna, deeply conscious of the atmosphere and the presence of the silent man at her side.

They sat down, and it was like being on a raft of silk gliding under the stars with the river lights glinting and the slow barges moving over the dark water. A hooter called, distant and sad, and was answered, and the Thames flowed on as she had flowed through London long before it was the vast metropolis it had become. It was magical and the wine that Slade poured into thin glasses was deliciously cool.

Suitable for what? she wondered suddenly. He had been here before. Had he brought Carmel? Or had he found this place for the one woman in his life, the faceless one about whom she had heard but never identified?

There was tension between them, but not the tension of desire. Anna held herself away from him, trying to avoid touching him. The unyielding set of his shoulders told her that he was not at ease. He regrets bringing me here, she thought. He wishes that I was that other girl . . . that other lucky girl, and he is sorry we came.

He moved restlessly and did not look at her, but she knew that he could see her reflection in the dark window. She had an absurd impulse to shout, "Say you hate me . . . say you love me . . . but for pity's sake say something!" but all she did was to sit and sip the fragrant wine.

He's angry, really angry, she thought. With me? With someone at the hospital or with himself? She felt a tremor of something resembling fear course through her, and fumbled in her handbag to give her trembling hands something to do. He glanced at her empty glass, and offered her more wine. "No, thank you," she said.

He raised his eyebrows. "I think this place is over-rated." He signalled to the waiter. "I want to talk to you," he said after settling the bill. "Shall we walk along the bank?"

It wasn't an invitation, it was an order and Anna braced herself. What on earth could he want to say that made his face into a mask of displeasure?

"I'd rather go back to Beattie's," she said, with more spirit than she felt.

"We talk first." He hurried along, taking one long stride to two of hers, and she was acutely aware of a wrinkled toe on her tights pressing on a nerve. By the time they reached a secluded spot by a high wall, where the buttress of the bridge joined it, she was breathless and indignant.

"I know what your sister means now," she gasped.

"Walking too fast for you?" His voice was cool and made no apology. He stopped and gazed across the water, pointing out landmarks as if he had to do a guided tour. Crisply, he talked of London, its history and its place in the lives of the hospitals there. Anna looked at him in amazement. Had he gone mad? And all the time he spoke, his voice held the same note of disciplined rage. "Yes, this is London, the city you said you loved. I remember you saying that there was no city like it and no place like Beattie's."

"I still say it," Anna answered defensively.

"Then why are you leaving? "He looked at her troubled face, and spoke more gently. "I thought that for you, the insidious charm of the place had done its work. I thought you had come back because you couldn't keep away, in spite of Rob Delaney, in spite of everything."

"I did," said Anna. "I love it all . . . but now, I have to get away." She looked out over the bank and watched a neon sign flash in the distance. The smell of the river, acrid and almost salt, met her nostrils, and she couldn't look at Slade.

"That doesn't make sense, unless you've decided to go with Delaney. I came back because I belong here . . . and for other reasons. But you haven't been back for five minutes and you talk of leaving."

"I'm thinking about it. I haven't settled anything. I have a theory that if one changes jobs frequently, it helps promotion. I suppose I'm as ambitious as the next, and I want to get on in my profession as much as you do in yours."

She knew she was talking too quickly and sounded very calculating, but she had to fill every scrap of dangerous silence. He was close to her and she could feel his breath on her hair, but his face was harsh and there was no warmth in his voice. "Every girl has a right to be ambitious," she said.

"*Ambition*? You come to us and think you can swan

off to fulfill some nit-brained whim?" He turned to her and gripped her shoulders, shaking her none too gently. "Ambition? And what about loyalty? What about friendships? What about that dedication you seemed to show? So it doesn't matter that you have begun to build a rapport with the team? It doesn't matter that Beattie's needs you? It doesn't matter that we all thought you were worthy of the job, the trust and the service you could give?"

"Stop it! You're hurting me. What right have you to tell me what I may do, where I should work or what I should do with my life?"

His fingers dug deeply into the soft flesh of her shoulders and his eyes were dark grey with pain. "Why, Anna? Why are you doing this to . . . us? What's wrong with other London hospitals? Guy's or Thomas's? The Middlesex? With your training and record you can get a job anywhere."

"I have to get away." Her heart was beating loudly and she was sure that he must hear it. "I want to go."

"*You* want? Anna Boswell has decided? You have to get away because everything didn't turn out quite as you wanted it to. Don't you ever consider anyone but Anna Boswell?"

She gasped. "That's a rotten thing to say!"

"But true. Aren't you really saying that you thought you'd spread the word that you were taking a job in . . . say Edinburgh or Bournemouth, and it's all a blind? Aren't you really saying 'bad luck, Beattie's, I'm off to Canada with Rob Delaney'? Isn't that what you really want?"

"Well, at least he loves me." Anna was nearly sobbing but she bit back the tears.

"Loves you? Ha! He isn't capable of loving anyone but Rob Delaney. He doesn't love . . . he uses. He drinks and he's not very pleasant when drunk."

"How can you possibly know?"

"I have eyes, my dear Sister, and Carmel talked to me." Slade's voice was curt.

"Well, she's prejudiced where he's concerned. He isn't exactly enthusiastic about her, either!"

"She said he's the most selfish man she's met."

"And she should know. She's met plenty!" said Anna. "Did she find you selfish? Or was it true what she was whispering so sexily, when you were draped all over her? 'Slade . . . you are the one.' I heard her. 'Slade, you are the only one'."

His fingers slackened their grip. "It was never like that," he said, quietly. "She relies on me as a friend. If you had been five minutes earlier, even you would have felt sorry for her." He frowned, recalling that Anna had visited her after he had seen her.

"She may say that Rob is selfish, but at least he cares about me. He sent me roses," she said, knowing it to be a lie.

He gave a sardonic smile. "So the way to Anna's heart is to send her roses. So, she's vain as well as selfish. My, my, what facets of your personality we're uncovering." But his tone became milder. "What makes you think he sent you flowers? Was it the bunch of rather nice red roses that you threw away?"

"Yes." She tried to walk away but his hand was on her arm. He took her to a seat and sat her down, none too gently on the rough wood. She sat with her hands on her lap and her feet crossed, and felt very small.

"When a man buys you very expensive roses, do

181

you invariably throw them away . . . even if you think they were sent by the man you love? Hay fever, perhaps?" he demanded sarcastically. "Poor flowers, they deserved a better fate. The man you love gave you flowers, and you fully intend going to Canada with him, and yet you destroy his gift? Strange creatures, women."

He looked down at her pale, stricken face. His mood changed to sadness. "Do you know, when I was a student, I wanted to send flowers to a nurse here, but they had no roses. Michael Johns wasn't running the shop then. I would have bought them even though they would have cost me the price of all my beer money for a month. If I had given them and found them in the trash can, I would have been bitterly disappointed . . . so perhaps it was better that I didn't send them."

He waited, but she made no reply. His quiet persistence was like that of an examining lawyer. "Why did you throw the roses away, Anna?" He paused then said softly, "Something upset you very much when you saw them."

The tension was there still, like a sheet of cold crystal between them. Anna gave a weary sigh. "I thought that Rob sent the flowers and was using them to persuade me to go back to him. I thought he imagined we could pick up the threads and begin again. I was furious." It was a relief to confess. She hung her head. "It was childish." She wriggled uncomfortably on the hard bench. "If you must know, I'm not going to Canada with him, now or at any time."

"May I ask what made you change your mind?"

"I didn't change it. I met him . . . at his request, and he tricked me into seeing him in London, but that was after I panicked and threw away the flowers, thinking that with them I'd be free of Rob, too."

"So the poor flowers suffered. What did he say when you told him what you'd done?"

"I asked him if he'd sent the flowers and he laughed. He boasted that he never sent flowers to women . . . he didn't need to do that. He said he gave flowers only when someone died."

"So you knew that Rob didn't send them. Who sent you red roses, Anna?" His voice was gentle, as if persuading her to ease her mind. He was probing for something that she wouldn't confess.

She looked up, startled, her heart beating fast. He was smiling and the corner of his mouth turned up in a crooked grin. "You surely don't think that Sir Horace sent them? Even Lady Ritchie would object if he sent a young woman red roses." He was teasing her, trying to keep his tone light, but hiding a much deeper feeling. "It never occurred to you that another man might have sent them?" She shook her head.

"You never gave a thought to your friendly neighbourhood surgeon?"

"You?" she breathed.

"Why not? Is it so impossible?" Slade spoke softly and his eyes held tender laughter. "So, you never gave a thought to me. Is it so strange to think of me giving roses to the woman I love?"

She started and gave a small cry.

"Impossible to imagine even if I thought she was in love with another man?"

"But, Slade . . ."

"Better," he said with approval. "That's the first time I've heard you manage to drag out my name. I began to think it was too repugnant for you to bring yourself to say it."

Anna sat quite still, her hands opening and closing on the glowing silk of her skirt. Slade took her hands and raised them to his lips. It was the kiss of a butterfly, and Anna trembled.

"I think we have a lot of explaining to do," he said tenderly, and kissed her lips.

"But you were in love with a girl at Beattie's . . . even while I was training." She half-whispered it, dreading that even now she would be second best. "Susan said that you were in love with someone, and used Carmel to hide the fact. I thought that you were trying to keep her away from Rob so that you could take her yourself."

"How could I bear to stand by and let Carmel take Delaney away from you, when I thought that you loved him? How could I watch Delaney break the heart of the girl I loved, even though it might mean my never seeing her again? I think that Carmel suspected my motives, and I was never sure if Delaney did too, but I never told a living soul."

"You loved me all that time ago?" Anna's eyes widened in wonder and a kind of humility, and he nodded.

"When you applied for the job at Beattie's, I thought that you must have recovered from your feeling about Delaney. It took courage to come back, my darling . . . so much courage. I rushed out and ordered roses as I imagined your loneliness. I wanted you to feel welcome and not to get cold feet and go away again. I thought so many things . . . I hoped and dreamed, and when I found the flowers in the waste-bin, I felt as if you'd pushed me into a very deep, cold lake!"

"But why didn't you say something? Why didn't you get angry . . . as you did tonight?"

"I was too hurt. I took it as the end of all my hopes; the ultimate rejection. I knew that Delaney was back and even if you had no idea that I had sent the roses, telling you at that point would have added to my humiliation. With Delaney back, I knew that it didn't matter to you if I'd sent them, Sir Horace had sent them, or even that repulsive youth with the spots on Lister Ward."

"And you saw Rob kissing me." He nodded. "And you didn't see my reaction to him! It was rather like me seeing just one aspect of your meeting with Carmel!"

"I couldn't bear to look too closely," he admitted ruefully. "Another minute and I might have hit him." He held her close and caressed the silk-covered shoulder. He kissed her with growing passion, leaving her weak and glowing.

"I didn't know," Anna said, "I didn't suspect."

"Sometimes you are the tiniest bit unintelligent, my darling, but I love you."

"Slade," was all that she could say for a while, as if she would never tire of hearing his name on her lips. Her heart was full and she knew that each, in separate dream worlds, included the other as the most important creature in the world. London droned on past them on the river and in the distant roar of traffic, and they were content to listen.

"Slade," she said at last, "what made you think that I might love you?" Her eyes were full of love and there was no doubts left in his mind.

"It was something that Susan said . . . a very devious, rather wonderful person is Susan."

185

Anna sighed. It fitted. She had never thought she could hide her feelings from her.

Slade took out a pocket-book from an inside pocket and opened it carefully. Inside was a red rose, pressed but still retaining its colour. "You see," he said.

"You kept one." Her voice was awestruck. "You kept one of the roses?"

His voice grew husky. "I thought I had lost you, having never really found you . . . you had touched it, and it was all I had of you."

She put her arms round him, drawing his head to her breast, and they held each other close, their coming together much more poignant because they had so nearly lost each other along the way. "You haven't said it," he said at last.

"Said what?" she replied dreamily.

"You haven't said you'll marry me . . . soon, please, darling."

"I love you, Slade," she said, simply. "I want to marry you so very much."

They linked hands and went to the car. "Having frightened the life out of you because you wanted to leave Beattie's, now I have to ask you to do just that," he said with grim humour. "Will you miss it very much, Anna? Am I worth it?"

"Oh, Slade, I hadn't thought of that, but it's a rule, isn't it? No husband and wife teams on the same unit." She looked upset. "Must I go? It seems so unfair, and just because I'm married doesn't mean that I'll be less efficient."

He frowned. "There are other theatres . . . not like the new one but there will be a vacancy coming up soon in the orthopaedic department."

He looked anxious, as if this might affect their happiness, then his face cleared. "There's another solution. Do you know the old house at the top of the hill? Sir Horace bought it and is having it gutted and refitted. He senses that private patients' wings in general hospitals might be phased out, and has made his own plans for a surgical nursing home near the hospital. I know he'd be pleased to have you in charge."

Anna drew away slightly and sighed. "I shall miss Beattie's."

Where had all her resolution gone? Where was the almost nun-like devotion she had professed for her work? She looked at the man at her side and knew that if he was at Beattie's, then she would still have a share in its life too.

"Cheer up," he said. "If you're a very good girl, I'll have a word with the old boy. Could you bear to live two hundred yards from Beattie's? With everyone you know from the unit coming in, and . . . me living in the flat there with you?"

"It sounds heavenly," responded Anna.

The city was behind them, the orange flashes of street lighting taking the place of the glinting river lights as they reached the nurses' home. They parked the car and went quietly into the hall. It was very peaceful, and Slade once more took her into his arms. "I do love you, Anna," he said.

They stayed in a close embrace, as if even now they couldn't believe all that had happened during the evening. Anna stirred and kissed his cheek. "We ought to get some rest . . . heavy day tomorrow."

He smiled. "I'm hungry," he said.

"You can't be! Or can you? Come to think of it, I am

too." She giggled. "How unromantic! I thought that girls in love never suffered the pangs of hunger."

"What is there to eat?"

"Toasted cheese?" she said with a roguish smile.

"No," he replied with a grin, "we don't want Susan coming down for some."

"We could eat it in my room."

"I don't think that would be wise." He kissed her gently. "I noticed some rather nice cream cakes in your room. I'll make coffee down here while you fetch them."

"But wouldn't it be easier . . ." she began.

His eyes were full of love and tenderness, the grey almost blue. "If I came to your room now, I would stay . . . I'm only human, and it's very, very tempting; but when I take my rose, I want it to be in church, and for ever."

Doctor Nurse Romances

Don't miss
December's
other story of love and romance amid the pressure
and emotion of medical life.

THE DOCTOR'S CHOICE
by Hilary Wilde

Nurse Claire Butler had been brutally jilted. How could
she trust any other man — let alone the one who had
warned her not to fall in love on the rebound?

Order your copy today from your local paperback retailer.

Doctor Nurse Romances

and January's
stories of romantic relationships behind the scenes
of modern medical life are:

TENDER LOVING CARE
by Kerry Mitchell

Stephanie loved nursing at the little Australian country
hospital, but why had Doctor Blair Tremayne suddenly
turned against her?

LAKELAND DOCTOR
by Jean Curtis

It was only when the beautiful Lena came to the
Lakeland village that Hilary understood why she had
stuck for so long to her job as Doctor Blake Kinross's
secretary!

The Mills & Boon Rose is the Rose of Romance

Look for the Rose of Romance this Christmas

Four titles by favourite authors in a specially-produced gift pack.

THAT BOSTON MAN *by Janet Dailey*

MY SISTER'S KEEPER *by Rachel Lindsay*

ENEMY FROM THE PAST *by Lilian Peake*

DARK DOMINION *by Charlotte Lamb*

**UNITED KINGDOM £2.20 net
REP. OF IRELAND £2.40**

First time in paperback.

Still available from your local paperback retailer